TWELVE MORE

By David Farrell

Also By David Farrell

The Last Resort

The Glove

You Can't Get Rid of Me That Easily

Twelve

Dropping the Belt

Printed in Australia
First Printing 2019

Paperback ISBN   978-1-64516-129-5

For My Mother

CONTENTS

HOME SECURITY

As technology advances, criminals will adapt and find new ways to commit the same crimes of old. That was certainly the case with Howard Smythe. He'd been carefully robbing houses for years with moderate success. Though the skill came to him late in life Howard excelled at it. Theft became something of a hobby, an activity to fill in his days now that he was retired. It kept his mind active, not unlike Sudoku. Howard was a patient and intelligent burglar, which kept him off the radar of the authorities. He could follow a target for days, learning their habits and routine, before he decided whether they were worth his time. He became so familiar with his target's lives that he could easily predict the safest and best window of time to break into their home. In most instances he'd found himself to be a natural.

Then a company called P.R.I.N.T. came along and made things difficult. The anagram came from the surnames of its five founding members, Perkins, Ronaldo, Ito, Nolan and Tanaka, each of whom had invested heavily. When the technology was ready, their business model was to install fingerprint scanners onto doors, replacing the need for key cards within a workplace. It began as a means for employees to enter safely and securely before some managers discovered another benefit. The thumbprint scanners would double as a way of confirming that staff weren't taking long luxurious lunch breaks, arriving consistently late or sneaking away early. Fingerprint technology wasn't new but for whatever reason it had a sudden surge of popularity. Managers could now hold their staff accountable for their time. P.R.I.N.T. decided to capitalise on the interest and move into the home security market by replacing house keys with thumbprint scanners. People upgraded their home security in droves and shares in P.R.I.N.T. went through the roof.

Howard had watched the trend with disgust. These scanners were impossible to cheat and had made his new career incredibly difficult. There had been other advances too. In the old days he might have just removed a panel of glass from a window to gain entry. Unfortunately for Howard windows had all been replaced by an almost unbreakable clear material developed in Germany. The average residence had become very secure. He knew he would have to adapt his methods or find a new pastime.

The only way to gain entry to a house was to be in possession of a person's fingerprints. Howard was not a violent man and his first idea, of severing a hand from a person's wrist, made him throw up a little into his mouth.

What was a safe way of stealing fingerprints? Perhaps copying them? he wondered.

Howard considered taking up a part-time job as a barista and removing prints from discarded coffee cups after use. There was no guarantee that the quality of a print would transfer and it seemed like a lot of work. After he obtained the fingerprints he would also need to find out where they lived – which would be difficult if he was halfway through a shift.

It became an annoying puzzle he couldn't solve. Howard started tailing people out of boredom. He followed them around mindlessly, watching as they pressed buttons to cross the street or call an elevator. People pressed with an index finger on some occasions and a thumb on others. He needed something consistent. The idea came to him while he was sitting in a public toilet. He heard a burst of air and was struck with inspiration.

The hand dryer.

Bathroom patrons willingly dipped their hands into the ravine of a hand dryer. The action was built into the bathroom routine. Their hands were usually outstretched and held still so the dryer could work effectively. Howard went home and ordered one online so he could investigate further.

It didn't take long for his plan to materialise. The hand dryer arrived in less than a week and Howard installed a small motion-activated camera into one side. During his research phase Howard loitered in an airport bathroom, washing his face, shaving, filling and refilling a drink bottle and brushing his teeth multiple times to avoid the suspicion of travellers. All the while he watched them use the hand dryers. He noticed that men would dry their hands the same way while facing the dryer. The device was idiot proof, with each man dipping his hands into the opening with their palms facing towards their torso. It would be very unnatural to bend one's hands the other way. There was no difference in technique and therefore no need to add a second camera facing the other way.

He tested his modified device – with his camera acting as a motion sensor. When Howard placed his hands into the dryer the camera took a burst of pictures. When he analysed them on a computer screen – in high definition – he could see the ridges and grooves of each individual fingerprint. From there Howard could replicate them. It was perfect.

Howard installed the device in a public bathroom under the cover of night. He felt proud of himself. If things unfolded according to plan the men he robbed would have no way of knowing how he'd obtained their fingerprints and perhaps, if he was careful, they wouldn't know he'd been in their home at all. With luck he could continue this game for some time without detection. His goal was to steal small but expensive items like jewellery, that wouldn't be immediately missed. Then, Howard hoped, the target would simply question whether they had misplaced the item. They might even blame themselves for its disappearance. He'd be slick and careful.

The next day he watched from his car and counted almost two hundred individuals that used the public toilet. That night Howard copied the images from the camera inside the dryer and found only sixteen sets of fingerprints had been photographed. Was it possible that such a large percentage of men weren't washing and drying their hands? Perhaps they favoured wiping the water onto their clothing or simply shaking the excess water away. *More variables to consider.* Another factor was the presence of a second air dryer. It was positioned on the wall next to the door. Howard realised another likely scenario was that men were using this dryer instead due to its location. He solved the problem by creating an 'out of order' sign and taping it to the second dryer. The next day he repeated his stakeout of the bathroom. The results had improved and he noted that he had almost fifty useable fingerprint scans. It was time to find a suitably wealthy target.

The next day as lunchtime approached he took up a post inside one of the toilet cubicles. Howard had packed a lunch and was in there for the long haul. He would sit and wait until he heard the hand dryer, then flush the toilet and walk out into the greater bathroom area to survey his prey. If the candidate seemed worth his time he would follow them at a distance for the remainder of the day. When his mark returned to their residence he would decide whether they were worth pursuing.

It was jarring to discover how many males visited the toilet and did not wash their hands. Howard would have felt extremely judgemental were it not for the fact that he was lying in wait to rob those conscientious enough to do so.

Flush…

Howard followed the first man to sanitise his hands back to his workplace. He manned the counter of a cold juice shop that closed at six that evening. Howard knew that if the juicer *was* the most promising lead that he could easily return and stalk him at closing time. He returned to his post.

The next few possibilities seemed untidy to Howard. He assessed their lack of style and determined on the spot that they were not worth trailing. He felt snobby for being so instantly judgemental but he had a sixth sense that he trusted above all else. Howard knew people.

As the afternoon began to drag, and Howard started to feel weird and a little claustrophobic about his surroundings, he heard the familiar roar of air. Someone was using the hand dryer.

Flush…

The man turned slightly as Howard exited the stall. He had a thin beard that had been lubricated with oil. His dark hair was slicked back and he wore a mid-range grey suit. Neither of them made eye contact but Howard sensed that the game was on.

From the far side of the street Howard observed as the man returned to his job at a phone store. He stroked his facial hair as he offered a customer the latest, and therefore greatest, product ever.

This one has potential Howard thought to himself.

The shop closed promptly at five-thirty. Howard, who was poised in the front seat of his car outside the shop, dutifully watched as the man climbed into a sports car. He knew he'd made the right decision.

The mark's house was two-storeys high and rendered in a dark shade of metal grey. It felt opulent, and distinct in this neighbourhood. Although Howard wanted to approach he exercised restraint. It was hard for him to make out any specifics about the home from a distance, or look for valuables through the windows, but he wrote down the address knowing he would return to the residence in the coming days.

Howard copied the target's fingerprints and set them aside for future use. He started to follow his mark – and gave him the alias *Steve*. Howard delighted in imagining a rich backstory for the man. He decided that Steve lived alone, which he'd verified by staking out his residence. Howard understood a man's need for solitude. Steve seemed to have a surprising amount of disposable income for a man in retail. In the evenings when he was home alone food would be couriered to the house. Steve fancied himself to be something of a playboy. When he wasn't at the gym sculpting his body – twice a week by Howard's count not including the hours spent doing sit-ups in his lounge room - Steve was bringing women back to his lair. Howard watched in awe as three different women – a blonde in a green dress, a rake thin redhead in leopard print and a second blonde in shimmering gold – entered his front door over three consecutive evenings. He started to loathe Steve for his easy success. Howard had never been married and still felt anxious talking to members of the opposite sex. Watching this house had stirred up long buried feelings for Howard. He'd been something of a nerd in school and had suffered beatings at the hand of people like Steve, the muscular ladies' man. Suddenly the impending robbery of this individual represented the tipping of the scales back into his favour. Steve was not only every bully from his youth but also every boss who'd kept Howard from promotion, every letdown in his adult life. The mission had become personal.

The best window of time for the robbery looked like around ten in the morning. Steve went to the gym two mornings a week – Mondays and Wednesdays - and then from there went straight to work. He decided that either of those days would be fine. If Howard avoided the nosy looking woman next door then walking into Steve's house would be a breeze. He manufactured the fingerprints onto disposable gloves. The prints were like a work of art. Howard smiled to himself.

I'm such a genius.

Monday came quickly and Howard parked his car two blocks away from his target. He watched closely as car after car zipped by him. He'd deliberately chosen a parking spot that overlooked the road that Steve would venture down on his way to the gym that morning. Soon the sports car headed north towards it's destination.

There he goes...

The game was on. Howard patiently waited until ten o'clock before striding out of his vehicle with his gloves and a dark ski mask. He walked at a slow meander towards the house. It was quiet now, as he expected it would be, and he tried not to draw any attention to himself. Howard scanned for neighbours and took a deep breath when he saw that the coast was clear. In a practiced motion he slid on his mask and turned ninety degrees to face the front door. In the twelve steps it took to move from the sidewalk to the door Howard slid both of the gloves onto his hands. If he made it inside he didn't want to leave a trace. He touched his thumb to the pad and watched the light turn from red to green. With a sigh of relief Howard slid inside and let the door fall closed behind him.

The air conditioning had been left on which made him wary. It wasn't a particularly hot summer but perhaps Steve preferred the cold. As he tiptoed past the entryway he spotted a camera overhead. He had anticipated this, as Howard knew the P.R.I.N.T system well. The feed from that camera would be linked to a hidden recording device downstairs. It would be checked in the event of a burglary such as the one in progress. Howard had disguised himself as a precaution. The recorders that P.R.I.N.T sold could only store 24 hours of footage at a time, meaning if everything went according to plan and if nobody realised he was there that any evidence of his crime would be erased by this time tomorrow.

The living area was incredibly dull to Howard. Every piece of furniture seemed like it came from the same mass-produced catalogue of trendy pieces. He'd been in dozens of houses just like Steve's. The living area flowed into the kitchen and Howard soundlessly followed the path. That was the moment he saw the dog.

It was a small bulldog that was asleep in a basket lined with pillows. Howard held his breath and cursed himself for not having any awareness of this canine until now. He managed to avoid the kitchen completely and, one step at a time entered the bedroom at the rear of the house. There were small hand weights on the floor. A double bed sat in the middle of the room. Howard found it very off-putting that it wasn't propped against any of the walls.

He rummaged through the wardrobe and the drawers. Single men usually hid their valuables in a sock drawer or under their bed. He found a collection of watches and decided on taking only two – the ones with the most dust on the boxes. He put them into his black cargo pants and moved on. He found a series of old basketball cards and assessed them quickly. Howard pocketed a Larry Bird, a Michael Jordan and what appeared to be a Shaquille O'Neal rookie card. Howard knew that men looked at items like this infrequently and it could be months before Steve noticed these were gone.

He found some jewellery that might have belonged to Steve's mother. Most of it was certainly ornamental and held no value to Howard but one piece appeared to have real diamonds. Howard had worked in a jewellery shop for a time and could identify the real thing easily. The diamonds were mounted on an old ring.

His mother's perhaps?

Howard pocketed the item, determining its worth at about seven thousand dollars, before moving on to the second bedroom.

It was almost completely empty except for a desk with a sewing machine and a pile of material next to it.

Could Steve, the gym junkie, enjoy sewing in his downtime? Or does this also belong to his mother?

All three of the desk drawers were locked. It was at that moment Howard heard the padding of dog paws against the kitchen tiles. He hesitated and wondered whether the dog would settle somewhere else. The curious bulldog could be heard scratching at the door only seconds later. He could smell Howard's presence but he wasn't barking.

Howard opened the door and let the dog approach him. On closer inspection he was an older dog and Howard thought he might have been going blind. Sensing that the canine wasn't going to trouble him he stepped around the dog and continued his search. He found a few more items of value that he thought wouldn't be missed for weeks. But soon he was interrupted as the bulldog started barking.

'Shhh… it's alright. Calm down boy.'

The barking persisted in a deep and repetitious manner. Howard made his way to the kitchen and the bulldog followed.

'Are you hungry boy? Let's give you something to eat.'

The fridge was full of prepared meals in matching plastic containers. Steve knew what he was eating for the next week or so. On the lower shelf Howard could see wrapped portions of meat that he assumed were for the dog. He grabbed one, unwrapped it and held it underneath the dog's nose with both hands.

'Do you want this?'

The dog was salivating at the idea. Howard placed it into the dog's bowl and noticed its name on the front.

'Good boy Rex,' he said as he gave the dog a pat.

The meat was boneless and after Rex had finished eating there wouldn't be any evidence that Howard had fed him.

Perhaps he was underfed. I certainly never saw Steve take Rex out for a walk. He's old but he still needs attention.

Howard felt better about his act of kindness as he approached the door to leave. The ring alone meant the heist had been a success, but he'd be able to fence the basketball cards through a dealer he knew. When Howard reached out to take the door handle he found that there wasn't one. In its place was a second P.R.I.N.T reader.

Why would this be here? Howard wondered to himself.

It was against regulations to have a thumbprint reader on both sides of a door. In an emergency – such as a fire - this would make it more difficult to evacuate. He'd read the operations manual, and this was irregular. Howard pressed his thumb to the pad but it did not immediately change from red to green.

He tried again with the same result. He pressed his other thumb and then analysed his gloves. The excess juice from the meat had soaked onto the gloves causing the ink to run slightly. Even though there was now only an infinitesimal difference between the print on his gloves and the fingerprint the reader was expecting it was enough. The gloves wouldn't work.

Howard skipped through the house and checked the back door. It too had a P.R.I.N.T pad installed on it.

What is going on?

Howard started to panic. There were no other exits and Steve would be returning that afternoon after he finished work. This was a problem that had to be solved without delay. Howard looked carefully out of the windows and cursed the German inventor that created this unbreakable material. The windows were bolted shut too.

Is that why the air conditioning is on? Steve never opens his windows?

He paced through the house and tried to think. Howard rummaged through the kitchen drawers and was surprised to find a set of keys. There were no keyholes on the front or back door but he took them and tried to unlock the windows without success. It was no use. Howard was sealed in.

He started to imagine the various scenarios that would transpire that afternoon. He had no explanation or reason to be inside this residence and would certainly be arrested. He'd been recorded on the P.R.I.N.T cameras, which meant that the evidence of his crime would certainly be found. He could attempt to overpower Steve and escape but Howard knew it was a battle he could not win. Steve was solid, and in far better shape than Howard. While he was deliberating the encounter, Rex the bulldog had passively made his way back to his basket and fallen asleep. He was oblivious to the trouble his feeding had caused.

Howard attempted to trick the P.R.I.N.T pad but it was increasingly reliant. Fingerprints are so small and unique that Howard would have needed to be Steve's identical twin to beat the system. He silently cursed Perkins, Ronaldo, Ito, Nolan and Tanaka for their ingenuity. He sat at the dining table and accepted his fate. He would probably be going to prison.

Although Howard had operated without detection for years this one slip up would unravel him. He would have to answer the question of how he got into the house. If he decided to be truthful his brilliance would be his downfall. They might even figure out that he'd been active for years and link him to some of his other ventures. He'd sold off a lot of the profits of his crimes but there were still some tell-tale items that he'd been holding onto. Some goods had been too hot to move right away. If he was discovered then a simple search of his place would lead to even more questions.

Then it occurred to Howard that the keys he held in his hand might be the keys to the locked desk. Maybe there was something he could use to escape. He moved quickly to the second bedroom and tried the keys one by one.

Success.

The top drawer opened to reveal a pile of black gloves.

The second drawer revealed more jewellery. Howard eagerly dove through the contents and found multiple high-end items. If he could escape now he'd have almost forty thousand dollars' worth of goods. This incentivised him even more.

The bottom drawer contained three pieces of material that had been cut into equal sized squares. There was a pair of thick scissors in the drawer too. The squares appeared to be part of a green dress, a patch of leopard print and another of shimmering gold.

It hit Howard like a semi-truck.

The pads were not a safety precaution at all. The reason the P.R.I.N.T pads had been installed on the inside was to keep guests in.

This house was a glorified kill room and Steve was a killer.

The three women Howard had watched him bring home had likely been murdered in this house.

It was like a soundproof cage. The windows were barred shut and the air conditioning ran all day to keep it liveable.

He would have gladly taken a trip to the police station and possible jail time over the grim alternative that he now faced. Even in the cool air Howard was now sweating. In a matter of hours he would have to fight Steve – or whatever his real name was – to the death. Unless he could convince him… or trick him… into letting him go. He could hide and wait for Steve to fall asleep, but without severing an index finger he'd still be a prisoner.

If Steve had gone undetected for this long he was probably careful, just like Howard. It was over. There was no amount of money he could offer Steve that would equate to the release that the homeowner would no doubt feel by killing him. A second glance at the contents of the fridge confirmed his suspicions. Rex had unknowingly helped to destroy the evidence of Steve's crimes.

Howard didn't like his chances of getting out alive.

THE FORMULA

When Brett looked at the topography of his living room he knew something had to change. He'd been living in LA for almost two years and the daily grind of writing his screenplay coupled with working as a waiter had been exhausting and time consuming. But today was different. Last night in a fever of inspiration Brett had completed his final draft of *Noni*.

He'd sent it to his agent and then immediately fallen asleep. Now, in the light of day, Brett realised it was time to clean up. He scooped up all of the takeaway boxes from his living area and recycled them. He played music while first emptying and then washing a sink full of dishes. He swept and then mopped the laminex floor of his tiny kitchen and put on a load of dirty washing. His burst of cleaning had timed perfectly with the total duration of Celine Dion's Greatest Hits. The morning was over but Brett was in a productive mood so he decided to call his mother.

'Hello honey, thanks for returning my call.'

'How are you feeling Mum?'

His mother June went into excruciating detail about the pain in her hip and how terrible it had been lately. She had been involved in a traffic incident involving a car that had run a red light and crashed into a bus she'd been on. The driver of the car had made contact with the side of the bus at forty miles an hour and then sped away. June had been sitting in the worst seat possible at the time. Her medical bills had started coming in and Brett was hoping if he could sell *Noni* that he could help her financially. The alternative would be moving back to Chicago to assist her in person.

'And how are you?'

'Really good. I finished my screenplay,' he said enthusiastically.

'Oh that's great dear. Was this the one about the man who laid an egg?'

'No… I gave up on that one. This one is actually about you and me.'

Silence.

'Mum?'

'You've written a film about me?'

'Well, yeah. It's sort of inspired by our relationship I guess. I mean… it's about how you raised me on your own and about the day I told you I was gay. I think it's really sweet. It's a drama and I'd love you to read it.'

'Okay. If you want me to read it I can.' Her tone was distant and inattentive, like she might have been spying on someone out in the street while simultaneously listening to her son.

'I'll send it over to you,' he offered.

'Fine, fine.'

Brett felt sure his mother would enjoy the story. He'd taken some liberties and made his mother much sassier than she was in real life. Noni, the title character, had long and hilarious speeches that Brett felt could be amazing on screen, if performed by a good actor. He'd sold two screenplays since moving to LA from Chicago with some of his actor friends. He'd lived with them initially but found their ongoing nightlife a hindrance to his writing. Brett found himself to be most creative late at night and didn't enjoy the constant interruptions when his friends brought home dates or stayed up working on their craft. Neither of his screenplays had been put into production yet but that hadn't stolen an ounce of his confidence or belief that this was his time.

If not now, then when?

He printed a copy of his screenplay for his mother and bound it with a blue cover page. Brett mailed it to her and went to Starbucks for a caramel latte.

The next day while he was trying to sleep in he received a call from his agent.

'I've got news. Are you sitting down?' asked Kyle. He was the kind of agent that literally participated in every fad he could. The kind of guy that let cultural trends dictate his life.

'I am,' replied Brett as he lay in bed.

'Nancy Michaels and her production company want to buy your script.'

'Nancy Michaels?'

It was a name that Brett hadn't heard in years. Nancy Michaels would have to be in her seventies by now. She'd been a star of the stage and screen for almost forty years but had become reclusive and disappeared from the limelight.

'I didn't know she was a producer,' said Brett as he collected his thoughts.

'She's been active for the last year or so. She's new to the investing game. Are you ready to hear their offer?'

'Yes.'

'Fifty thousand dollars. That's your end *after* I take away my fee. I had them build in my twelve percent so I could give you a nice round number. How good is that?'

The figure was nothing to be scoffed at. The deal also gave him a very small percentage of the film's box office, should it turn a profit.

'And she wants to *make* my script? Not just put it in turnaround?'

'Absolutely. This might be the start of something bigger for you too. If *Noni* gets made then studios might greenlight your other presold scripts. It could be a snowball effect. And if we can point to a produced work then I'll have less trouble getting you in the room for your next one…'

Kyle may have been bullshitting Brett but it felt good. Brett hadn't expected the response to be so positive and immediate.

'Can I meet her?' he asked. Brett wanted to know that his script was in good hands.

'I'll set it up!' replied Kyle enthusiastically. Brett could *feel* him grinning through the phone.

On the following Wednesday Brett was picked up in a town car and taken to the residence of Nancy Michaels. It was a mansion in a gated community that boasted patrolling guards on horseback, which was highly irregular for suburban Los Angeles. After the car moved through the gates Brett saw rows of lush flowers and huge palm trees marking the path to her door. The house was beyond impressive. Brett felt like he'd wandered into another world.

This is what success looks like.

The driver knocked on the door and Brett was passed on to an assistant that led him through to a greenhouse at the back of the mansion. In a wicker rocking chair, facing away from Brett, was Nancy Michaels. Brett followed the assistant to her side and was introduced.

'So you're my writer?' she asked with a wrinkled smile.

'It's a pleasure to meet you Miss Michaels.'

'Please, call me Nancy.'

'Nancy. Thank you.'

'I loved your script. I've been reading a lot of them lately and there's nothing out there quite like it.'

'Thank you. That's so nice to hear.'

'So tell me why you wanted to meet with me Brett. And I don't want to haggle with you. My price is final.'

'Oh Miss Michaels I would never…'

'It's Nancy. If we're going to do business you had better be able to call me *Nancy*.' She looked very insistent.

Brett hesitated. He hadn't really met anyone famous before this moment.

'Nancy… your offer is very generous. What I wanted to know is whether or not you'll actually be *making* the film. I've sold scripts before and they've been put on the backburner. I suppose my concern is… I want to see my words on screen.'

'You want a screen credit?'

'More or less. I'm just after assurances that this isn't going to end up in a drawer somewhere.'

Nancy Michaels smiled a wide smile that proved she was still, even in her seventies, one of America's sweethearts.

'I don't have a lot of time left. If you sell me your script it will be in production within three months. That's a promise. And God willing we'll both be present at the premiere.'

They shook hands. Brett called Kyle and told him to make the deal.

Nancy started casting the film immediately. For an older woman she seemed to have no shortage of mettle. Within a week she'd called in favours and organised a working crew. The film had a shooting schedule and even an approximate release date. Brett couldn't believe his ears when his phone rang one day and a film critic from *Rolling Stone* magazine asked for a comment about the production.

Things seemed to be going swimmingly. Brett was feeling amazing. He called his mother and updated her on the project.

'So who's going to play me?' she asked.

'I'm not sure. And you know it's not actually *you*, right? It's a woman named Noni. She's just an amalgamation of you.'

'But she's still based on me?'

'Yeah. And the son in the movie is still based on me.'

'Well it's nice that you're keeping busy.'

'And Mum, I've got good news,' said Brett.

'What?'

'I'm coming to visit.'

Brett packed a bag and travelled back to Chicago to see his mother. When he saw her hobbling towards the door he realised that her condition had become worse. She struggled to give him a hug before sitting down on her floral sofa. Brett made her a tea.

'So I got some money from my script and I was thinking that I could use some of it to hire you some help while you recover.'

'I'm not an invalid dear.'

'Of course not. But I wanted to help. I'll take care of these bills and maybe we can hire a service. Someone can pop in and help a little. Or a cleaner?'

'I'm capable of cleaning.'

'Well… if you need a hand.'

'Perhaps.'

Brett had caught her during a particularly bad moment. June had struggled to find sleep the night before and doubled her pain medication without telling anyone. She might have thanked her son for his generous offer but she was having trouble focussing.

Brett was at the local shop buying his mother low fat milk when his phone rang.

'Hey man… jut wanted to give you a heads up,' said Kyle.

'What's going on?'

'Everything is still totally on track, but I just have to tell you that Nancy is altering your script. Just a bit.'

'She's *what?*' Brett felt his collar tighten around his neck.

Kyle explained that Nancy Michaels had spent some time rewriting Brett's script, which now featured revised dialogue. He assured his client that he'd still be getting the writing credit, although it might end up being shared with her.

'Can I read it?'

Kyle agreed to send him a copy.

'But that's not all.'

'What? What else has she done?' Brett felt helpless as he faced the dairy aisle, hundreds of miles from Hollywood.

'She's going to play Noni herself.'

Brett cut his trip to Chicago short and read the reworked screenplay on his flight home. He was sitting next to a curious woman who kept interrupting him during the flight.

'So do you work in the *biz*?' she asked.

'A little. I'm a writer.'

'What have you done? Anything I would have seen?'

'No. Nothing yet.'

'Are you Brett Carson?'

He was surprised to hear his name come out of this stranger's mouth.

'How do you know my name?'

'It's right there on the front of the script.'

Brett looked at the front page of the screenplay. It now read:

Noni

By Brett Carson & Nancy Michaels.

'Do you know Nancy Michaels?' asked the woman, poised to hear any celebrity tidbit that was on offer. On second glance Brett considered that his travel companion might have been an aspiring actress.

'Not very well.'

As it turned out Nancy had changed his screenplay just enough to share the writing credit for it. Brett needed to speak to his collaborator as soon as possible.

Nancy Michaels agreed to meet him at an exclusive lunch spot in West Hollywood. She arrived ten minutes late, which did not bother Brett as much as he wished it would. After drinks were ordered he tried delicately to get some answers from Nancy.

'Well, I had a read of the latest version of *Noni*,' he started.

'And what did you think?'

'I was surprised to be honest. I noticed you are now the co-writer…'

Nancy Michaels smiled.

'And I'm sure you've heard that I'll be playing the lead role? It's been in all the tabloids.'

'Yes.'

'That was my primary motivation when I bought your script Brett,' she replied with a smile.

'But…'

'This is the business,' she continued, 'and we're both going to profit from this. You'll be able to walk into another writing job, or sell another screenplay off the back of this.'

'And you're definitely still making the film? It's on track?' he asked.

'Yes, of course.'

Brett wondered if he'd signed a kind of deal with the devil. He'd now be sharing credit with Nancy Michaels, and in return he would have his first screen credit. It wasn't ideal but she was right, they would both benefit from the arrangement in the end.

'I'll be casting some big names in supporting roles as well,' she continued, 'in order to secure the Academy's attention at award season.'

'It seems a bit premature to assume this will be nominated for awards,' stated Brett.

'On the contrary, it *will* be nominated… it's just a question of categories.'

'What are you talking about?'

'I want to win an Oscar before I die. Your script is currently the best vessel for me to achieve that goal this year. If I'm in the film then I can be nominated for my acting and if my name is on the screenplay then I'm doubling my chances, aren't I Brett? If I'm the Producer too maybe we will find ourselves up for Best Picture selection as well.'

He was dumbfounded. The sheer confidence that she would be nominated for an Academy Award – for a film that hadn't been made yet – astounded him. He didn't want to criticise her, or inform her he thought that she was getting ahead of herself. Instead of demanding she should see a doctor and have her head examined, which is what he was thinking, Brett found himself saying nothing at all.

'The important thing is that your film will be made. That's what you wanted isn't it?'

'Yes…'

'You worry too much Brett.'

'This is all so strange,' he said, finding his voice, 'How can you… *know*… so surely that the film will be worthy of these accolades?'

'There is a formula to these things my dear. And I've been studying it.'

'You have?'

'Yes of course! I have an Emmy Award, a Tony Award and a Grammy. It's just the Oscar I need now.'

Brett left the lunch in a daze. When he Googled Nancy's accolades he saw that she was given her Tony Award first, for her work in the production of *Memphis Undertow* during her mid-twenties. She'd also directed and starred in the play. *Was she hedging her bets even then?* Her Grammy Award was a baffling case. Her name was attached as a co-composer on a track that won Best Original Jazz Composition, before the category was phased out. Further research implied that she may have only inspired the work, as her name was not attached to any other song or musical work that Brett could find. Her Emmy was awarded in the 1980's for a guest role on a drama. Nancy Michaels had worked in the industry her entire life. If she was sure his screenplay would amount to an Oscar, who was he to argue? Brett decided the best course of action was to let this unfold under her careful and experienced direction. *Who didn't want an Oscar?*

The Hollywood tabloids reported on the production constantly. Articles were picked up by minor news outlets and Nancy Michaels was interviewed every two weeks on average. She spoke eloquently about the story and how proud she was of *Noni*. She never mentioned Brett by name in any of the publicity. It was a whirlwind of activity for her and a breeze of melancholy for him. To compound things Brett found he had writer's block. His agent Kyle attempted to get him a job as a writer on a sitcom but his ideas fell flat in the room. He was asked to turn in a spec script but he couldn't wrap his head around the situational comedy.

To make matters worse Brett found out that the general consensus was that the public believed the story was actually *about* Nancy and her son, who had died over a decade ago from a drug overdose. The press speculated that *Noni* was some kind of love letter to what might have been.

On set Nancy was the queen. She commanded respect as the lead actress, cast minor celebrities and friends in bit parts and ruled the production as its chief financier. The Director, who was a critically acclaimed European, seasoned in dramatic filmmaking, seemed to consult Nancy on every shot and camera setup. Brett could see he was one of many pawns and that she was practically directing the film herself. He wondered why she didn't attach herself as a co-director, but was afraid to ask. Perhaps her winning formula required her to specialise. Maybe too many roles would somehow dilute things in the eyes of Academy voters. He smiled and nodded in the corner near the craft services table. Nobody asked him about the script. If an actor had a question about the dialogue they consulted Nancy. His silence had been bought for fifty thousand dollars.

Brett only watched a few days of the filming before his mother June took a fall in her garden and he flew back to Chicago to see her.

'How's the film coming?' asked June, her leg now permanently elevated onto an ottoman.

'It's interesting,' he said with a shrug. 'Not like I thought it would be.'

'You didn't think it would be interesting?' his mother asked.

'No… I mean… I did. I guess I didn't know what to expect.'

'Well that might be because you've never been on a real film set. It's bound to be different.'

'It is?'

'Well, you've been sitting in a dark room writing. It's different when the words are coming to life.'

Brett's mother had been a featured extra on a television show in her youth. The equivalent to a model that holds up prizes to the camera. It was hard to explain the evolution that had occurred between her career and his. Instead he nodded and made himself a cup of tea.

He didn't return to Los Angeles for several weeks despite the beckoning phone calls from his actor friends. None of them had been upset when Brett couldn't even get them an audition for *Noni*, but they were sure he was missing out on a life experience by staying away while his script was being filmed. They assured him that he would regret not being there. Brett shifted the blame to his mother, claiming that she needed him, but the real reason lay with Nancy Michaels. She'd sent him an email letting him know that everything was going according to plan and asking him to contact her if he was planning on visiting the set again. It felt like he was being cautioned, as if the party he was attending had suddenly uninvited him. There was a foul taste in his mouth now. His film was no longer his own. Nancy Michaels was changing it, and Brett was afraid of the beast it was evolving into.

In the lead up to the premiere Brett was asked to speak about his screenplay with Nancy. The event was held annually by the Writer's Guild of America and the audience was mostly comprised of film students and hopeful screenwriters. Nancy had declined the appearance but Brett, knowing some of his peers would be in attendance, was keen to speak. After his acceptance he received a call from Nancy.

'You can't speak at that event,' she commanded.

'Why not? I'm a writer and it's just another promotional opportunity, isn't it?'

'They'll ask you about me.'

'So? I know what to say,' replied Brett.

'Things are in motion here. This is not required of you. It's not in the formula.'

'Not required of me? Maybe you should send me a list of what is required. This whole experience has been very weird Nancy. I don't know what you want from me.'

'You've already done your part. I just want you to attend the premiere and smile for the cameras. Otherwise that meeting you have at NBC might get cancelled.'

Through Kyle he had arranged a meeting with the head of development at NBC to brainstorm ideas for a new TV show. It was odd that Nancy knew about this deal, as he had been sworn to secrecy about it.

'Is that a threat?' Brett could feel himself getting red in the face.

'I don't make threats, deary.'

Brett decided he wasn't afraid of Nancy. Frustrated, he kept his appointment with the Writer's Guild as planned. When he turned up and shook hands with the host he was informed that he was no longer required and that they had booked another writer for the slot.

Nancy was like a disease. True to her word she somehow made the executives at NBC cancel his upcoming meeting. They were extremely apologetic, citing that they wanted to go in 'a different direction' but it was painfully obvious who was pulling the strings.

With the premiere approaching, magazines hyped the film with Oscar buzz and featured many of the supporting cast and crew in favourable articles. Nobody contacted Brett's agent to book him and nobody called for a comment or a quote. In a haze of dark inspiration he wrote a screenplay about a Hollywood actress that is captured and tortured by a former fan. A kind of modern retelling of *Misery*. It was an incredibly unsellable story, because of the heavy torture, but it made Brett feel better. He printed a copy and stuck it in a drawer; like a letter that was written but never sent.

The premiere was held at Mann's Chinese Theatre in Los Angeles. Brett had flown his mother out for the event. June had to be aided by a crutch but was in good spirits. While Nancy was extremely busy with publicity she did make sure to say hello to Brett and his mother on the red carpet.

'So you're Brett's mother then?' Nancy asked.

'I certainly am.'

'The real Noni.' whispered Nancy.

'You might say that.'

'Loosely based on…' chimed in Brett.

'You must be very proud of your son. He's a terrific writer.'

'I am indeed,' a beaming June replied.

Brett smiled. It was a touching moment.

'Thank you Nancy, that's very nice of you to say-'

'Enjoy the show,' she said, interrupting Brett and moving along down the line of reporters.

The film itself played perfectly. Nancy had seen the potential of it on the page and whipped up an Oscar worthy film that everyone would be talking about. The experience was made extra special for Brett, whose mother cried audibly throughout the film's climax. She held her son's hand for the majority of the two-hour screening. It was a raging success and the film received a ten-minute standing ovation – which the press exaggerated out to fifteen.

For your consideration notices were taken out and on the morning of the nominations Kyle phoned his client.

'Are you sitting down bro?' he asked.

It was still early and Brett was in bed.

'Yeah.'

'You're an Academy Award nominee my friend! Congratulations! Remember to thank me if you win, okay?'

The film had been nominated in two categories: Brett and Nancy for Best Original Screenplay while Nancy Michaels was also nominated for Best Actress. He couldn't believe it. She had predicted it perfectly with her formula.

Brett's friends threw a party for him and Kyle fielded several writing offers. Brett now had enough money to get his own place and bring his mother out from Chicago to stay with him.

The press continued to hype the film, and the comparisons to Nancy's deceased son intensified. Brett had been told not to talk to the press but they continued to approach him.

'What's the big deal?' his mother asked. 'Why don't you just answer their questions?'

'They think the film is about Nancy and her son. If they find out it's about me and you they might not care about it… and then it will be my fault that Nancy doesn't win an Oscar.'

'So you're avoiding the spotlight?'

'I mean… she's been right about everything so far. I can't talk to anyone. Not yet,' replied Brett.

June didn't know whether her son was being sensible or not. She enjoyed being in Los Angeles, and ultimately was just pleased with his good fortune.

'I just want you to get the recognition you deserve. You wrote that script. I read it, before Nancy Michaels went and changed it. She didn't improve it one iota. It was perfect before that.'

Brett had considered arbitration; the process that determines whether writing credit has been earned. In the end he decided not to proceed with it and just share credit with Nancy. Winning an Oscar was one of his biggest dreams and now that it was a possibility he would behave himself. He declined all media requests and started working on a new screenplay about a former marine that becomes a children's entertainer. He isolated himself from his friends and started staying up late into the night.

That meant that June heard the breaking news first.

She woke her son and explained that Nancy Michaels had suffered a fall and entertainment news channels were reporting she was in hospital. When he turned on his phone he had several missed calls from Kyle.

'It's true man,' his agent confirmed. 'She fell off a ladder or something. Her people haven't publicly confirmed anything but they have told me… off the record… that she won't be attending the Oscars.'

The Academy Award ceremony was the following night. Everyone was talking about Nancy's fall. It dominated the news cycle. Brett, who had brought his mother to the event, was forced to repeat the same sound bite for each and every media outlet.

'We're all praying for Nancy to make a speedy recovery.'

He had no information about her condition and had been told he wasn't allowed to visit her. There was a genuine concern that this might be the end of Nancy Michaels.

When the nominees for Best Original Screenplay were announced June leaned over and whispered to her son.

'Congratulations.'

'I didn't win yet Mum.'

'Yes you did. Just look around.'

She was right. On this night Brett was being praised for his writing. Nancy had been right too. Brett had secured many more writing jobs thanks to *Noni*. During the applauses he realised that he was doing what he loved, and he had Nancy to thank for it. His mother took his hand as the winner was read.

'And the Oscar goes to… *Gretchen's Banquet*.'

It was bittersweet for Brett, who found he was crying. He didn't see the camera and unfortunately his tearful face would later become a meme – claiming he was a sore loser. It remained popular for about a month on the Internet. Brett ignored it and eventually it went away.

In the category of Best Actress Nancy Michaels secured herself an Oscar, completing the fabled EGOT. Against all odds she hurdled one obstacle after another until she achieved her dream. One of her producing partners read a brief statement on behalf of Nancy before she was applauded endlessly as a sweetheart of cinema.

A week later Kyle called Brett with some news.

'It's Nancy, she's awake. She's being discharged from hospital and she wants to see you.'

'That's excellent.'

Brett made the journey to Nancy Michael's mansion as soon as possible. He was excited to see how she was doing and congratulate her on the Academy Award. The flowers looked more beautiful than ever as he headed up the driveway. A different assistant led Brett to the same greenhouse at the back of the property, where Nancy sat in her favourite wicker chair.

'I'm so glad you came,' she said with a smile.

'How are you feeling Nancy?'

'Oh as well as ever.'

'What did the doctor's say?' asked Brett.

'There were no doctors, deary,' she replied. 'That was a ruse.'

'A *ruse*?'

'A distraction. A ploy. A marketing method… a way to get *Noni* over the line. I'm only sorry you didn't get a statue too.'

Nancy indicated to a nearby shelf where she had positioned her brand new Oscar next to all of her other notable awards.

'You didn't fall?' he asked.

'No. What would I be doing on a ladder at my age?'

'I can't believe it.' Brett was genuinely shocked. Nancy had given the performance of her life, on and off the screen.

'It all worked out for the best. And you didn't do this for the award, did you? You wanted to see your story on the screen.'

Nancy was right again. He'd written the script for his mother June, as a way of saying thank you for her support. Brett had wanted to tell her he loved her and this was the easiest way he knew how. She'd beamed at him when she'd accompanied him to the premiere. His mother had loved watching Nancy breathe life into her story on screen. It didn't matter that the audience thought it was Nancy's story. June knew it was hers. In a roundabout way it *did* find its intended audience. It wasn't really about awards or fame until it was.

As his career continued Brett Carson had to do press retrospectively for *Noni*. It didn't matter what project he was working on, he was forever linked with the actress. Every year or two he'd find himself on the end of a question about what she was really like, or how the experience of working with the late Nancy Michaels had changed him. Whenever he was faced with a question like that he regurgitated the same sound bite over and over again.

'She was an amazing actress and I'm so lucky to have known her.'

'Careful, that's delicate,' said Julia's Grandmother as she passed over the cream coloured box.

'Oh, thank you.'

Evan watched his girlfriend from his position on the sofa. He was totally bored with the exchange. He wondered what would happen if he jumped up and shook the box violently. Obligation forced him to attend Julia's birthday party but soon he would be free of this commitment. Evan was planning on ending their relationship after the party.

Julia carefully unwrapped the gift and smiled at the gathering of relatives who were in attendance. Her parents, who had been divorced for almost a decade, were putting on a brave face for the occasion. They were both sceptical of Evan at first, but over the past six months had changed their tune. Julia was increasingly happy and that was all they could ask for. Evan scanned the room. He vaguely recognised her aunts although he couldn't remember their names. Nobody else looked familiar.

'Wow...' said Julia, peering inside the box. 'Um... what is it exactly?'

Her Grandmother shifted past several guests.

'Take it out of the box dear,' she said with a wave of her hands.

Julia lifted it out.

Once it was unfurled it was clearly a necklace. Evan rolled his eyes, assuming his girlfriend hadn't been able to tell due to the additional packaging that had surrounded it. The jewel at the centre was a red ruby, and the ornate golden chain gave Evan the feeling it was very old.

'That pendant has been in our family for seventeen generations,' she said proudly.

'Whoa! That's a lot!' replied Julia. 'And the chain?'

'No… the chain is newer. I had to replace the old one years ago.'

'It's beautiful, thank you so much.'

Evan looked at his watch. *How much longer do I have to put up with this?* he thought to himself.

Julia threw him a smile and hesitantly he returned it.

Cake was served and speeches were made. Julia's mother read an entry from her childhood journal about wanting a daughter of her own. There wasn't a dry eye in the house, with the exception of Evan. He was counting down the minutes before he could escape.

'Are you having fun?' asked Julia, when they were alone in the kitchen.

'It's a… party,' said Evan with an indifferent shrug.

'So I was thinking this summer we could go and see my father's boat. It's at his place in Byron Bay and he's been asking me to visit for ages…'

'Um… maybe. I don't know,' he responded.

'Have you ever been to Byron Bay before? It's really nice.' Julia had a habit of touching Evan when he wanted to be left alone. As she spoke she rubbed his arm and tried to touch his face. It took a lot of willpower for Evan to resist recoiling from her. Julia's white cat Turnip brushed himself against Evan's leg. He hated that sensation. Suddenly he felt claustrophobic. It was all too much.

I have to do this now.

'Listen Julia…'

'What is it?'

'I didn't get you a present,' he said.

'Oh that's alright. I'm just happy you could drag yourself away from that video game you're developing. It seems to be taking forever!'

'Well, it's a lot of work. You have to build a whole world you know.'

'It all sounds kinda boring to me. But you know I hate video games,' said Julia.

'But video games are my life.'

'Sure… for *now*. But you're going to graduate and get a real job after that.'

'I don't want a *real* job… I mean… video game development *IS* a real job,' he said, a little thrown.

'But a job traditionally…'

'What?' asked Evan.

'A real job usually pays the bills…' Julia folded her arms.

'When the game is finished and someone buys it I'll make a lot of money.'

'That you'll have to split with Henry.'

Henry was Evan's roommate. In truth they were both living in Henry's mother's basement rent-free while they tried to make a game called *Werewolf Strike*.

'So?'

'So,' she continued, 'is that all you want out of life?'

'No… I mean… I'm happy. '

'You're happy pretending to be a werewolf in your downtime? That's what you want?'

'Yes.'

Julia rolled her eyes. Evan exhaled in frustration.

'I think we should break up,' they both said at almost the same time.

'Wait… *what*?' he said. Evan was sure he was getting the jump on her and was feeling shocked that they were somehow on the same page.

'Hang on… you want to break up with *me*?' asked Julia.

Neither of them dealt with the revelation well. There was shouting, followed by Evan ineffectively punching a wall and marching home. The party was ruined.

Later, in Henry's mother's basement Evan wondered if he'd just made a terrible mistake. It was different when he thought *he* was ending the relationship. Now, in the wake of learning that Julia was unhappy with him, it was starting to sting.

'Forget about that bitch,' said Henry, his dark hair sweeping across his brow. 'We've got work to do!'

Henry and Evan worked into the night on *Werewolf Strike*, exchanging ideas for the forest level. It was a nice distraction to have, but it wasn't enough. Julia lingered in his mind, refusing to leave Evan's thoughts.

In the morning he called her and asked her to have lunch with him.

'No,' she replied, almost instantly.

'No? You don't want to see me?' asked Evan.

'Of course I don't. We only just broke up!'

'Come on! Meet with me,' he pleaded.

'I said no.'

'We could talk…'

'We're talking now! What do you need to talk about?' she demanded.

'I just don't like the way we left it.'

'You broke up with me at my birthday party Evan.'

'That's not fair! You wanted to break up with me too!'

'You know what? I was right to want to end it. You are a shitty guy Evan! You can't help yourself and you transform into this… this *monster*. You're just like the stupid werewolf from your game. You ruin things and then you can't even remember the damage you've done!'

Julia swore at him and hung up the phone.

Evan was morose for the remainder of the week. When Friday night arrived Henry forced Evan to go out clubbing. They had four shots of tequila each and started to dance. It was a well-worn recipe for the boys and they revelled in knowing exactly how much alcohol to drink in order to have a good time. They found a group of women and Henry started chatting one up. He was good-looking and Evan was a little jealous of how easily women warmed to him. The music was loud and he couldn't hear what they were saying but Henry kept pointing to her top, which had an octopus on it. Evan felt like a third wheel so he wandered away from their conversation. When he passed the bar he spotted a woman sitting all by herself. He decided to take a chance and open his mouth.

'Oh... hi...' he said, bumbling to get his words out.

'Hi,' she said. The woman was not a natural blonde, her regrowth revealing her as a brunette.

'Sorry... I don't want to bother you. See that guy over there?' asked Evan, pointing at Henry.

'Yeah?'

'That's my buddy. He's just hitting on that girl... and I didn't want to cramp his style.'

'Well, sit with me. Just while you wait,' she said as she moved her handbag.

It felt easy. He'd been welcomed to a seat at the bar at the expense of his friend's reputation. Evan chatted to her for a while before Henry returned, having struck out with the octopus enthusiast, and the two went to another club.

At the new venue Henry started chatting to another girl almost immediately, which led Evan to execute exactly the same play on a new target.

'Hey there... *sorry* to bother you... do you see that guy dancing over there?'

'Yeah I see him,' his new target replied.

'That's my buddy. Do you mind if I sit with you while he chats up that girl? So I don't look like a loser all by myself?'

'Sure.'

Evan tried several variations of the same move, finding it even more effective when he made fun of Henry or himself. It was suddenly fun being single again. At the end of the night he'd found someone to go home with and Henry had not.

'I'll see you in the morning,' Evan promised as he shook Henry's hand.

'Proud of you man. See if she has a friend for me!'

'I will.'

Evan walked out of the club feeling like a champion. He'd secured this angel in a mini skirt through skilful conversation and seduction. He didn't even care that Tina was so obviously drunk. He tried to see past the worn lines on her forehead. Evan needed this. They stumbled away together towards the promise of her residence.

'Where exactly do you live?' he asked.

'Thiiiiis way…' coaxed Tina, dragging him by the arm.

As they walked Evan started to feel sick. He worried that he'd overdone it at the bar. He'd bought a lot of extra drinks to continue some of his 'spontaneous' conversations, which meant he'd consumed more alcohol than usual.

'Come on,' his date called, pointing across an oval. 'It's just over here.'

He stumbled over and felt his whole body start to shake.

'Are you alright?' asked Tina.

Evan couldn't answer. As the full moon appeared from behind a cloud his forearms were suddenly coated in hair. Evan's jawline fell and his teeth grew in his mouth, almost doubling in size. He could feel his bones stretching and he could barely concentrate as the structure of his body morphed. It was incredibly painful and he let out an involuntary howl. He saw a look of horror on Tina's face. She started to run away from him just as Evan blacked out.

It was the daylight that forced Evan from his slumber. He rolled over and found that he was lying in a carefully manicured garden in front of a retirement home.

Evan couldn't work out what was leaving such a bad taste in his mouth. The mystery was solved when he saw Tina's corpse. Her torso was in pieces and the more identifiable segments of her were scattered in the garden bed. The smell of flesh forced Evan to vomit, and he was shocked to see that the colour of his bile was a bloody red.

Evan started to recall the events of the night before. He remembered the transformation more clearly in the light of day although he still couldn't focus on anything afterwards. He'd changed into something horrible and lost control. Looking down he now noticed the rips across his shirt and pants. They would never be worn on a night out again. There was literal blood on his hands.

Tina's blood.

Evan ran home as discreetly as he could. It was still early and his path was clear. Henry's mother had provided them with a key to the back door, which led through a laundry and a second bathroom before snaking its way to the basement. This entry point meant that Evan and Henry never crossed paths with their landlord, keeping them akin to downstairs neighbours in an apartment building. Neither of the boys were ever bothered by her as she lived alone upstairs and liked her solitude.

'What happened to you last night? Did you hook up with that older bird?' asked Henry as Evan arrived home. Henry was lying around in front of the TV. Evan didn't respond, surprised his friend was awake at such an early hour. He slipped into the bathroom and locked the door. Henry was there in a flash.

'Bro! Open up. I want the deets!'

'Go away man.' Evan peeled off his clothing and jumped in the shower. His friend gave up after he heard the water running.

When he was done scrubbing away the blood in the shower Evan examined his naked flesh in the mirror. He didn't look like a monster, but he had certainly started feeling like one. Even though he couldn't remember killing Tina, it was there… somewhere in the back of his mind. The memory just couldn't be unlocked.

Evan decided to confess everything to his friend, including his transformation into something monstrous. Henry was confused by the admission.

'Is this some kind of angle?' he asked.

'What do you mean?' replied Evan.

'Is this… like a new *level* in *Werewolf Strike* or something? Are you pitching this to me?' Henry toyed with his Grandfather's gun as he spoke, even though he'd been told it was a priceless war artefact. Henry liked to think it inspired him, like the baseball bat did for Tom Cruise in *A Few Good Men*.

'No! This really happened!'

'You turned into a werewolf?'

It sounded ridiculous to say out loud. Last night he had taken the form of a werewolf and murdered Tina. *But how?* There was a full moon last night, but that had never changed him before. The image of her decapitated head could not be erased. It turned out Henry was no help at all. He kept rambling about bonus levels where the virtual werewolf in their game collects bones instead of coins. What had changed since the last full moon? Evan hadn't altered his diet, or anything that he could think of… except for ending things with Julia. He had to see her.

As Evan waited outside the University library where Julia was tutoring he considered his predicament. Was this transformation something that had always been dormant inside of him? Was the monster waiting to come out? Perhaps the excess amount of alcohol had activated something. Maybe he was a superhero and this was his unlikely origin story. He spotted Julia and his heart sank. Who was that guy she was with?

'JULIA!' he called across the quad.

She spotted him immediately and started walking faster. Evan raced to catch up.

'JULIA!' he called again, a little louder.

Julia stopped walking and as Evan approached he could hear her apologising to her handsome acquaintance.

'Can we talk?' asked Evan when he was within earshot.

'What are you doing here? You're embarrassing me.'

'In front of your new boyfriend?'

Julia looked offended by the accusation.

'You broke up with *me*. Don't tell me who I can and can't date,' she replied.

'We broke up at the same time!'

'It doesn't matter. We're not together anymore.'

Evan squinted at her new beau.

'So you're dating this guy?' he asked.

'No!'

'Is that true buddy?' Evan asked the man, who ignored him completely.

'What do you want? Closure?' she asked.

'I need to talk to you. Something's happening to me,' said Evan.

'Yeah something's happened to me too. I've grown up. We're done Evan. Go back to your basement.'

It was a cheap shot, and so Evan sunk to her level.

'I cheated on you,' he said quickly.

'What?'

'I cheated on you… twice… with your friend May.'

Julia was shocked, which made Evan feel like he was winning. He had completely forgotten that he had turned into a werewolf and torn a person apart just one night earlier. This felt more important than anything else.

'When?'

'We were texting for a while and when you and your family went to the snow I told her she should come over.'

'And you had sex with her?'

'Yeah. Twice.'

'You're an arsehole Evan. You've never been a complete human, have you? You don't know how to be decent and compassionate… and REAL! I hate you. Don't you ever call me again!'

Suddenly, as she started to walk away, Evan remembered the true purpose of the meeting.

'Oh wait! You don't understand-' he started before she interrupted him. Julia angrily clasped her birthday necklace, which had bounced forward out of her cleavage during her sharp turn.

'Stop it Evan! You're a monster... but you already know that, don't you? And you'll have to live with that forever. But I don't have to hear about it. Stay away from me. I'm serious!'

Julia and her male companion walked away, leaving Evan feeling like a dick. The truth was he'd never had sex with May, but she had come over and they'd fooled around a little. He'd wanted to do more but he'd stopped himself. Now he wished he could go back in time and cheat on Julia properly.

The news reported Tina's death as the work of an animal, such as a bear, and nobody suspected it was Evan. Convincing Henry that he was capable of transforming into a werewolf and going on a murderous rampage proved an ordeal. Evan decided that the best way to show his friend would be to wait until the next full moon.

When the time came Evan persuaded Henry to stay in for the night, promising an all-night session of work on their game.

'If you buy the beer this time!' Henry was easily motivated by alcohol.

The two mapped out a level where the heroic werewolf character is trapped on a submarine and has to fight his way out before the vessel is submerged too deeply. If the player could murder his captors before the time limit ran out and escape then they'd move on to the next part of the game. When the two were satisfied that they'd done enough Henry suggested sharing a joint outside. Evan knew in his heart that the moment he went outside he'd lose control, turn into a werewolf and possibly kill Henry beneath a buoyant moon.

'I need you to do something for me man,' said Evan.

'What's up?' Henry replied.

'I want to walk outside by myself first… if I change into some kind of monster that will give you more of a chance to run away.'

'Not this again. I told you that must have been a dream. Maybe you smoked something you shouldn't have?'

'I hope you're right Henry… but just in case you're wrong can you please do this for me?'

'Fine… but after this I don't want to hear any more about it, okay?'

'Fine.'

Evan walked out into the backyard by himself. Henry couldn't wait and started smoking in the doorway. It was a cool night but Evan didn't notice the chill. He found the moon, peeking through a number of clouds, and concentrated his attention on it. Right away he felt his breathing intensify. His jaw became slack and his teeth stretched out from inside his mouth. It was happening.

'Get out of here Henry!' he called, waving his now fur-covered arms to usher his friend away.

'What the fuck…?'

The cigarette fell from Henry's mouth as he turned and slammed the door behind him. Evan doubled over, clutching his body as it jutted out against him. He couldn't stop the transformation now. Evan closed his eyes and felt the all too familiar feeling of blacking out.

When he found his bearings again Evan's first thought was for his friend. He found himself alone outside, this time leaning against a tree, with torn clothing and blood stained pants. He felt hungry, and prayed that meant he hadn't killed anyone this time.

'Henry?'

Evan hoped that if Henry was alright that he now believed in whatever dark magic was plaguing him.

When he entered the door and travelled down to the basement he was thrilled to find his friend in the corner of the room.

'Henry! Thank God!'

His friend was pale.

'Evan? You're… *you* again?'

As he approached he saw the gun in Henry's hands. He must have feared for his life and taken up his Grandfather's weapon. Evan still couldn't remember anything.

'It's me. Are you alright?'

'I locked myself down here in the basement. I was fine…' replied Henry with a distant look in his eyes.

'That's great. I'm sorry but I thought it was the only way to-'

'My MOTHER on the other hand wasn't so lucky.'

Henry raised the weapon and pointed it at Evan.

'Hey man… easy…' said Evan, lifting his hands up defensively.

'You killed her. She's in pieces upstairs.'

'I'm… so sorry… I don't know what's happening to me. I didn't have any control over it…'

'It doesn't matter,' said Henry as he started to cry. 'She's gone.'

Henry cocked the gun.

'Don't shoot me man! I don't want to die,' pleaded Evan.

'Do you think *she* wanted to die? She let you live here rent-free and *this* is how you repay her? My mother was a good woman. You're going to die.'

'I thought you were my friend Henry! I thought you were going to help me figure out why this is happening to me!'

'No… the reason you showed me the real you last night was because you knew that I was the only one who could free you. You and I are werewolf experts, and you couldn't kill yourself.' Henry kept the gun trained on Evan.

'What are you saying?'

'Last night I melted everything I could find that was 100% silver. It took ages but I managed with my welding kit. Everyone knows that the only thing that can kill a werewolf is a silver bullet.'

'Henry, please I-'

It was too late. Henry fired the gun, propelling the homemade silver bullet directly into Evan's forehead. He fell to the floor instantly.

The attack should have killed him but it didn't. Evan was perplexed when he woke up on a silver gurney in the city morgue.

Why didn't I die?

He considered that perhaps werewolves were not in any way hurt by silver, or that it was an old wives tale, but he was in human form when he was shot. He found a reflective surface and looked at his forehead. There was a hole. Evan took his index finger and pressed it knuckle deep into the fresh cavity.

He felt no pain.

Am I dead? Is this heaven? Or hell...

The morgue looked tidy. There were no other bodies in the room, but there were several human-sized drawers where Evan suspected bodies could be kept. He slid open the nearest one and saw a naked man who had been operated on recently. He had been examined and sewn closed. The man had no obvious smell, which concerned Evan. He expected the stench of death to be overwhelming. As he looked at the man he found he had started to salivate.

The fleshy corpse in front of him was suddenly, and unexpectedly, looking appealing. Evan had the urge to bite the man, just to see what he tasted like. He forced the man's head to one side, which was difficult due to rigor mortis, and chomped his teeth into his neck. It was a juicy sensation but it was missing something. Evan considered that the experience would be improved if the meal were fresher. He needed to find someone to satisfy this new hunger. He needed a warm body.

Realising he was famished Evan hopped up and onto his feet completely naked. All that he could think about was quenching his insatiable bloodlust. Through a series of doors he came upon a man eating a sandwich in a break room. He ran toward him, delighting in his shock and screams, before biting down into his pulsing neck.

That's better.

He drank until the sandwich enthusiast collapsed on the tiled floor. When the man was certainly dead Evan's mind cleared. He was able to focus once more. He realised that he was naked first and stripped the dead man of his clothes. His white shirt was so stained that it appeared red so he didn't put it on. Instead he found the man's jacket hanging behind the door and wore that instead. He walked barefoot out into the day and found his senses heightened. Evan could feel a surge of energy worming its way through his veins. But where to go next? Evan couldn't go home. Not after his friend had shot him in the head. If he went back now there would be another fight, and more blood would be on his hands. He decided not to pursue Henry and murder him, despite the fact that a part of him wanted to. If the situation were reversed Evan might have reacted the same way. But why was he still alive? He had no right to be.

Evan found himself in possession of a dead man's wallet, complete with credit cards. Evan decided he would be less conspicuous if he had a shirt and shoes. After finding himself some suitable attire Evan headed towards Julia. He was hopeful that despite their last interaction she would still help him.

As night fell Evan became tired. He could feel his energy fading away as if he was powered by the sun itself. He recognised the unfortunate truth: he was hungry again.

It seemed he needed to eat every twelve hours or so in order to maintain himself and prevent turning into a mindless zombie. While he waited outside her house Evan spotted Julia's cat and felt himself starting to perspire.

Could I eat a cat?

He barely considered this question before breaking Turnip's neck and draining his lifeless corpse. It felt like he'd just had an energy bar.

Looking in the window of her house Evan watched as Julia undressed for a shower. Her body looked delicious to him in two ways now. When she was out of sight he made his way around the perimeter of the house. He didn't want any witnesses in case things went south. That's when he saw a man sitting in the living room. It was the guy Evan had accused of being her new lover at the quad.

What's he doing here? Do they live together now?

Evan was furious. He took the spare key, which was still in the same place underneath the fake stone, and let himself into the residence. Evan crept up behind him and without thinking about the consequences bit the man on the neck. His victim was stunned. Evan took a second bite. Julia's new lover was dying, his mouth failing to make a sound. The shock was too much for him to react at all. Evan didn't let go. He didn't care what kind of relationship they shared. Seeing this man in Julia's place while she took a shower pushed him over the edge. Evan held onto the man until he was deceased. Then, as though he was possessed by a demon he fed on the man, slurping and smacking at his flesh, until he heard the shower stop.

Shit.

Something inside him made him panic and run away. He couldn't control himself when the thirst and desire for a drink kicked in. He knew enough about zombie lore to realise what he now was. Evan remembered dying at Henry's hands. He was something else now. He was devolving into an undead creature.

Evan had just murdered a man but he surprised himself by feeling almost no remorse. That part of him, the part that should feel empathy and crave forgiveness for his selfishness seemed to have died. *Did he still have a soul?* His needs were primal now. He stalked his prey in the streets, dining only under the cover of night. He would lurk in public spaces such as parks and alleyways, striking only when his hunger reached its peak. After a week of feasting on the flesh of his community Evan didn't recognise himself anymore.

It was an encounter in a public bathroom that changed everything. Evan had felt the need to eat and located a target walking alone on a Thursday night. He was presentable, dressed in a suit and tie, but staggered as if inebriated. He was the obvious choice and Evan didn't hesitate when the stranger went into a public toilet alone. He crept into the bathroom, knowing that if his target had additional company he could certainly dispose of them too. Evan's hunger made him strong. The man was standing alone at the furthest urinal. He was not urinating, instead facing Evan, eyes vacant and dim. Evan approached the figure cautiously but he did not budge. *What on Earth was he doing?* It looked as if he'd fallen asleep standing upright. Evan felt a sudden and overwhelming need for flesh, causing him to bite into the neck of the man, who still did not flinch.

This sensation was different for Evan, who likened it to eating something sweet and filled with sugar. He was absorbing the life of the man but it was supplying him with a different kind of high. He could feel it pulsing through his veins to his fingertips. Evan closed his eyes as he fed.

What was different about this man?

When Evan was satisfied and his pulse had slowed he stood and looked at himself in the mirror. The blood that he'd taken from this man was a dark green colour that had the consistency of sewerage. He looked down at the corpse beneath him and saw the man's face now looked like a sultana, all wrinkled and misshapen. This had not been a man at all.

There was a low rumbling outside akin to a small earthquake. Without thinking Evan hopped outside to check it out, fearing that it was a police helicopter that had finally caught him mid-kill. In actual fact it was a grey disc that he identified as a flying saucer. Evan had only moments to accept the existence of extra-terrestrial life before he felt himself rising through the air towards the craft.

In a nanosecond he found that he'd materialised in a room that he could only assume was inside the craft. He felt uneasy, and despite the trip taking no time at all his body felt as if it still needed to adjust. He was alone for perhaps ten seconds before a creature appeared in front of him. Evan had no idea where it had emerged from, as though he'd blinked and during that time it had arrived. It was wide and the base of its body was made of layers of dark green ring shapes, piled up like a stack of car tyres. The blobby torso became thinner at the top and a worm-like arm stretched out to examine Evan.

'What are you?' he asked, trying to evade the limb as it propped forward.

'What are you,' it repeated, mimicking his tone and inflection.

'Tell me where I am,' demanded Evan.

The blob creature in front of him began to change shape. Evan watched as it remoulded itself into the form of a human being. The man standing in front of him had the appearance of an older gentleman, which made him feel at ease.

'Can you understand my words?' asked the man.

'Yes,' replied Evan.

'Is the volume I have selected acceptable for you?'

'Yes.'

'Good. I must ask you how you came to be here,' the alien enquired.

'You abducted me! I didn't ask you to!' shouted Evan, surprising himself with his frustration.

'Modify your volume.'

'Please put me back down! Return me to Earth.'

'That would be quite impossible. We are currently travelling over a million miles from your planet and to venture back to those coordinates would be against our directive.'

'And what is your directive?' asked Evan.

'The Loinparths have been summoned,' he said calmly.

'What is a Loinparth?'

'The Loinparths are my people. We have been contacted due to an invasion on our home world. All Loinparths are returning to prevent the Stol from taking over our planet.'

Evan tried to comprehend the mass of information that he was now in possession of. This *Loinparth* creature in front of him had effectively kidnapped him from Earth and they were now hurtling through space towards the Loinparth home world, which was about to be attacked by Stol... whatever that meant.

'I just want to go home,' he said. 'How do I get home?'

'My foremost concern is determining how you got here. Could you repeat your actions prior to your removal from your... *Earth*?'

Evan was hesitant but decided to be honest. He described his zombie-like hunger as a disease that was attacking his body. He spoke eloquently about the way he'd lose control and feel an impossible urge to devour others in order to quench his appetite. He told his captor about his most recent kill in the public bathroom, and waited for him to respond.

'Can your confirm that my comrade, the man you attacked, is now deceased?'

'Yes, I believe so.'

'The solution presents itself. You are currently in possession of my comrade's life force. It resides in you. This explains the manner of your removal from your world.'

'You thought you were beaming up your friend?'

'Certainly. His departure presents a new issue in that my comrade will no longer be able to partake in our upcoming battle. Do you wish to substitute?' asked the alien in human form.

'Do I wish to substitute? In battle? No thank you. I don't even know what a Stol is.'

'A Stol is the natural enemy of the Loinparths.'

'I understand that,' replied Evan, 'but I mean… it's not my war.'

'This information is irrelevant. You will fight alongside the Loinparths or you will be disintegrated. Do you wish to substitute?'

Evan was out of options and so he cautiously agreed to fight, hoping that the situation would change. The spaceship settled into the Loinparth's galaxy within the hour and Evan was instructed to be ready for battle.

'What kind of creatures are the Stol?' he asked.

'The Stol are slow but solid orbs that are hardened by their many eons of fighting.'

'So… are you saying they'll win? Are the Stol going to defeat your people?'

'Due to their genetic composition and combat experience I would say that the outcome is inevitable.'

'Then what are we doing? Why are we fighting them at all? Shouldn't we be running away?'

'I would ask you not to raise your volume again. The Loinparths are an ancient species. We understand that if this is to be our ending we would rather rise together or fall together. Things will be as they should be.'

Without warning they both began their transition from inside the craft to the surface of a new planet, which Evan had to assume was the Loinparth's home world. The planet was covered in craters and although the environment seemed uninhabitable Evan found he had no issues continuing to breathe. He didn't even know whether he still needed to breathe as a zombie.

'This is where I leave you,' said the alien who remained nameless.

'Why? Where are you going?'

'We are going to fight. Follow as you can.'

Without waiting for a response he shape-shifted back into a dark green tyre-worm creature and scuttled towards a nearby rise. Evan, feeling underarmed and underprepared, followed closely behind. Perhaps a fate worse than disintegration would be this Loinparth leaving him alone in this desolate place. Across the horizon Evan noticed a siege already in progress. The Loinparths were fighting against smaller egg-shaped creatures that resembled upright rocks. Neither side carried weapons and Evan watched in horror as the rock creatures – which had to be the Stol – brutally ended the lives of several Loinparths. The Stol were stronger and more mobile. Even though they were rounded masses they had the ability to bounce up and crush the Loinparth army to death.

Evan heard a noise behind him. As he turned he saw a second brigade of Stol rolling towards them, flanking their rear. They were trapped, which meant running away was now impossible. Evan was struck by a Stol and tumbled to the ground. Then, in a precise movement, one shot down and crushed his chest.

As his enemy rolled on Evan sat up.

Of course that didn't kill me. I'm already dead.

He stood up, surprising the nearby Stol creatures, and then started to fight them with his bare hands. He punched and thrashed as best he could but the damage he was inflicting was minimal. After only a few strikes he was once again knocked down and crushed by a member of the Stol legion. After each crushing they would assume, rightfully so, that the force would render Evan deceased. Against all odds he continued to stand up and resume with his ineffective hand-to-hand combat.

Eventually, through a stroke of luck and persistence, he cracked open the shell of one of the Stol. The interior was rubbery and as Evan learned, delicious. He feasted on this alien life form, which gave him a delightful and weird burst of energy. If his immortality proved permanent he assumed he would be able to continue fighting until he dispatched the entire army, but he didn't know how long that would take. Evan also worried that by the time he killed and ate all of the Stol fighters, there might not be any Loinparths left to take him back to Earth.

It was during that selfish concern that Evan spotted a moon in the distance.

Could it work? Evan wondered to himself.

He focussed all of his energy on that moon, thinking back on his second transformation in front of Henry. He visualised himself becoming a werewolf in his mind's eye.

It was working…

The familiar transformation took place immediately and Evan felt his skeleton shifting, and his fangs growing. His heart beat faster as fur appeared through his pores. He looked up and howled in agony before he lost himself and turned into a monster.

When he regained consciousness he was once again on board the alien craft in the same vacant alien room as before. His head ached and he was disorientated.

'What happened?' he said.

Evan sat up and realised he was alone.

'Hello?' he called.

His cry summoned the same alien presence that he had interacted with previously. He waited patiently as it transformed into its human form. It smiled a small smile, which was different.

'You have risen,' he stated.

'Yeah… what happened out there? I can't remember,' said Evan as he rubbed his temples.

The Loinparth alien explained that the Stol army had been defeated, largely due to Evan's contribution.

'Is the ability to re-configure your body mass a common attribute among your kind?' he enquired.

'No… in fact I can't explain why it's happening to me.'

'Regardless of its origins, your other form-'

'It's called a werewolf,' interrupted Evan.

'Your werewolf form was beneficial to our plight. I am pleased to report that the Stol forces were destroyed in their entirety.'

'I killed them all?'

'Yes.'

'Wow.'

'You are being celebrated as a warrior. I have been instructed to deliver you to Ul-rung, which is known as the paradise planet. There you will remain for the rest of your natural life.'

'Can you take me back to Earth?' asked Evan.

'You do not understand. Ul-rung is a more desirable location.'

'You're not going to understand this… you don't seem to have feelings.'

'The Loinparth people feel as one.'

'Look… while I was asleep… or unconscious just now I had the weirdest dream. I remembered when I was a teenager and I-'

'What is *teenager*?' asked the alien.

'Oh… um… like when I was a younger man. In my teenage years.'

'Proceed.'

'So when I was a teenager… a young man… there was this dance that they made us do at school.'

'You were forced to participate in said dance?' enquired the alien.

'Yeah… and there was this girl named Violet that nobody wanted to touch. The guys would have to rotate their dance partners and whoever had to dance with her wouldn't hold her hands. It was peer pressure; do you know what that is? It's when other people dictate what you do… your behaviour…'

'Why have you been dwelling on this particular memory?'

'Well it bugs me… you know? I should have just held her hands when we danced. I don't know why I didn't. I don't know why everybody treated her that way. We were just kids… being stupid I guess.'

'In retrospect you would have modified your behaviour?'

'Yeah… I think I would have danced with her. I would have treated her like a person you know? I'll bet she felt awful.'

'Despite the possibility of ridicule from your peers?'

'Yeah… because she got really hot. She became a model and travelled all over Europe. We were all wrong about her.'

'And your kind are not often wrong?'

'We're always wrong… I've been wrong a lot lately. That's why I need you to take me back to Earth. Let me go and see my girlfriend… ex-girlfriend Julia. I need to tell her I'm sorry. I lied to her… I treated her badly. I should have just been honest. If there's time, I'd like to fix it.'

The alien once again pitched the benefits of living on Ul-rung before succumbing to Evan's request. They travelled back to Earth and the alien spaceship was able to locate Julia, using Evan's memories. The alien in human form said goodbye to Evan and he was teleported into Julia's room. It had changed.

Was this a different house?

Evan knelt down by her side and shook Julia, who was asleep in her bed.

'Evan?'

As she sat up he saw various tattoos on her neck and hands. Her hair was shorter but her face was as beautiful as ever.

'Julia! I'm so glad to see you,' he said, throwing his arms around her. 'You look great.'

'What are you doing here? How did you get here?'

'It's such a long story… I was a werewolf, and then a zombie and I guess most recently I was an alien. It's been… a lot.'

Julia sat up in bed.

'I have to tell you something Evan. I think it's my fault.'

'What do you mean?'

'I think I did this to you. I accidently turned you into a werewolf… and I guess I made you immortal.'

Julia explained that she was a witch, and that her powers had been activated at her birthday when she was gifted that necklace.

'I come from a long line of witches.'

'You do?'

'Yeah. I didn't mean to but I think… I think I *cursed* you. I'm sorry Evan, I was really pissed off… and we'd just broken up…'

'I get it. I mean… it's a lot to take in but I get it.'

'So you're immortal?' she asked.

'Yeah, I keep on coming back.'

'I'm immortal too,' replied Julia.

'How do you know? Have you died?'

'Evan… you've been gone for over a thousand years. In that time everyone you and I knew died. The entire landscape of our planet has changed. Everything is different now.'

'Are you serious?'

Julia nodded.

'Look… I came here because I wanted to apologise,' said Evan.

'You did?'

'Yeah. I never cheated on you with May… that was a lie. I love you. And I'm sorry I ended things with you at all. I should have fought for you Jules.'

'Thank you for saying that,' she said with a smile.

'I mean it.'

'Have you been thinking about this for a thousand years?' she asked.

'I guess I have,' Evan replied.

'And you've been thinking about me? About *us*?'

'Yeah,' said Evan.

'Me too.'

EAVESDROPPING

She's home.

But she's alone this time. Where's her boyfriend tonight?

I hear the familiar sound of keys landing in a metal bowl and Harriet dumping her bag on the table. Or is it a chair? I can't be sure.

I've been living above her for a week now and in that time I've worked out some of her routine.

She's your classic nine to five girl; at least she was this week. Harriet sounds like one of the good ones too. I heard her calling her mother on Monday night. They talked for over an hour but I could only hear some of it.

I don't like her boyfriend though.

He sounds like a dick.

It's just my impression of course… you never know what people are like when they're alone. But he's dismissive in the way he treats her. He doesn't stay the night. I don't think he loves her.

Not like I do.

I know that's crazy. I know how it sounds. But there's something about her. She sings sometimes when she's by herself. It's mostly old Motown songs too, which means she's got good taste.

Harriet is an old soul.

I hear her shuffle around and I wonder what it would be like to meet her. Would we be friends? I like Motown too.

Suddenly she's on the phone and I strain to hear her conversation.

'Becky? It's Harriet… yeah… I just needed someone to talk to.'

What's happened? Is she alright?

'It's Shane. He's been cheating on me.'

I knew it! Her boyfriend is a dick!

'Yeah… you were right.'

Looks like I wasn't the only one who thought so.

'So he told me he wanted to learn French, right? Remember he was taking those classes?'

Is she sitting down? Perhaps with a glass of wine in her hand? Or is Harriet the kind of girl that likes to pace when she's on the phone?

'Well I wanted to surprise him with a trip to Paris. So I've been secretly learning French too.'

She's smart. And she's not afraid to try new things. Maybe I should learn French. Then when we meet I'll be able to sweep her off her feet.

'I had to tell Shane about the trip because I need him to get his passport ready… and take time off work. He needed to be in the loop.'

Oui is yes… that one's easy. Madame is lady, isn't it?

'And I told him in French… and I totally surprised him. He couldn't understand me. And at first I thought maybe his French class wasn't very good… or he wasn't picking it up…'

But Shane was doing something else wasn't he?

'Shane met a girl… yeah… he met someone else… and the French class was a cover. He's been screwing her every Tuesday and Thursday night.'

What a dirty piece of shit. Fuck Shane.

'I know… I know…'

You deserve better Harriet.

'And so now I've got these two tickets to Paris and I can't even imagine going.'

Her voice is breaking. She must be devastated. It sounds like Harriet only just found out about the infidelity.

'It's the city of *love* Becky… this was supposed to be a romantic trip. I mean… how could he do this to me? To us?'

I'll go with you Harriet. Forget about Shane…

'Oh God…I just remembered Arthur's wedding. Shane and I were supposed to go together.'

I love weddings. I'd like to meet your friends. This is perfect…

'I suppose there were signs. Shane didn't always want to have sex. I just figured we'd been together a while and that was sort of natural, you know?'

She was oblivious. Blinded by love I guess.

'Nobody's cheated on me since High School. Remember Mario? Yeah… the soccer player. Oh, you didn't know about that? Well you weren't the only one…'

Why do so many men cheat anyway? Can't they appreciate when they have someone great right in front of them?

'Yeah… so first Mario and now Shane. Maybe I need to take a break from men for a while.'

I don't think you need a break. I just think you haven't met the right man for you yet. You haven't met me.

'My parents could use a trip to Paris. They've never been and their wedding anniversary is coming up in May.'

Harriet is so sweet. She's generous and nice… and I can't believe that Shane cheated on her. I would never do that.

'Anyway… sorry to unload on you like this… I know you've got to work in the morning.'

How can I feel so strongly about someone that I've never met? Is there something wrong with me? Or is it some kind of kismet, maybe?

'Thanks Bec… I'll talk to you later… yep… okay… thanks… bye.'

I should go down and meet her right now. I should just introduce myself and let the chips fall where they may. What's the worst thing that could happen? She tells me to get lost? Sure. But what's the best thing that could happen? Harriet looks into my eyes and we find out this connection… this unspoken thing that is happening… is real.

That's what I want. I want someone real.

She's turned on the TV now. Maybe we could watch something together. Harriet could tell me about her day… about how Shane is the worst… and I could nod and rub her feet. She'd smile at me and tell me how good my massages are getting.

I'd tell her about my break up. Frankie and I were serious too. We were living together and I thought we'd be together forever. I told her that I wanted to marry her. Frankie didn't love the idea.

Sure... it had only been eight months, but sometimes you just know it's real. You extrapolate the relationship out in your mind and you can visualise the rest of your lives together.

Frankie wasn't so good at seeing the bigger picture.

So I moved out.

From the sounds of things Harriet and I would be well suited. We've both been hurt in the past and it feels like we'd be stronger together. I'd treat her like the princess she is. I'd take her on the trip to Paris... and I'd never turn down her affections.

'Hi Mum.'

She's on the phone again. Nothing much on television I guess.

'How's Dad?'

She's selfless. Harriet's so great. I'm glad Shane's out of the picture.

'Can you ask him for the number of that exterminator you used? I think I have a mouse or something.'

It's not going to be easy but if I set my mind to it I know I can win her heart. Money is tight at the moment but maybe I can make her a gift. I could write her a poem or a song. Maybe a mix tape?

'Could you lend me the traps then? I saw like... twelve or so in Dad's shed...'

Harriet. Such a beautiful name too.

'Mum? I've got to go... that's Shane on the other line...'

What does he want? I don't like the sound of this...

'Shane?'

Oh no. Suddenly I'm seeing my future with Harriet disappear. She's going to backslide into Shane's arms and the window of opportunity will be closed.

'No... you don't get to say that to me. You're the one who's acting like an idiot.'

You tell him Harriet! Kick him to the kerb.

'Why? Whatever you have to say you can say it to me now.'

Fuck you Shane. Tell him to fuck off!

'I don't want to see you. You can come and get your stuff another time... because I don't want to talk about it anymore.'

Things are looking up after all. She's no fool.

'You really hurt me, you know?'

Of course he did...

'I don't know...'

Don't forget he cheated...

'Fine... fine... yeah? Well... come over then.'

What?

This will not do. If they reconcile then Harriet and I won't have a chance! What's wrong with her? Is she drunk or something? She's letting Shane come over. Maybe she's not as smart as I thought she was. Or maybe she needs closure. When Frankie and I ended it I needed closure too. I'll admit that I kept track of her. I wanted to make sure we were really done. Maybe that's what Shane wants. Just to close the book once and for all.

I can hear her taking a shower. The water is pulsing around through the pipes in the walls. She wants to smell nice for him. She's considering taking him back.

It's not over with Shane.

I'm becoming invested to this soap opera that's unfolding one floor below me.

Harriet's probably putting on make up. If I could only see her I'd know. I could find the look in her eyes that revealed her doubts about Shane. I wish I could talk some sense into her. He doesn't deserve another chance with you!

But of course here he is, knocking loudly enough that I hear him. What an inconsiderate guy...

'Hey,' he says.

'Hi.'

I hear Harriet's door close and it makes me nervous. He's a predator and she's invited him in.

'I need to apologise to you,' says Shane.

'Yes you do.'

'I'm sorry. You need to know that she didn't mean anything to me.'

'Why did you do it then? Did you think I wouldn't find out?' demands Harriet.

Good for you... stand your ground...

'No... I guess... I panicked. I'm glad you found out actually.'

'You are?'

'Yes. Harriet... losing you made me realise what we had... what we still have. I still love you.'

'That's not good enough Shane.'

'I've hurt you and I'll never forgive myself for that. But I can't stop loving you either. So if you want me to leave… that's fine. But I won't stop fighting for you.'

'Are you crazy? You cheated on me.'

Yes he did.

'I know. It was a mistake. I hope one day you can forgive me,' says Shane.

Harriet is so quiet. What is she thinking about?

'I've missed you,' she says, finally breaking the silence.

No!

'I've missed you too.'

More silence.

'I need you to leave Shane… before I do something I'll regret,' says Harriet.

'I don't want to leave. I want to stay with you.'

'That's not a good idea. Please.'

'I'm not going anywhere Harriet. We still have things to talk about.'

'Just go. If you love me you'll leave me alone. Please.'

Go away Shane! Harriet doesn't want you here.

'I'm staying. I don't want to lose you.'

He won't listen. I'm going to have to go down there and rescue her. Harriet needs me!

'Shane…'

'No. There's something here. We're worth fighting for.'

Is she crying? She is! I have to help her…

'What the HELL was that?' asks Shane suddenly.

'I heard it too,' says Harriet.

Oh no…

After someone slides a chair across the ground my hiding spot is flooded with light. I see Shane's face as he grabs me. His firm hands around my collar subdue me and he drags me through the hole in the ceiling and into Harriet's living room.

Harriet looks quite beautiful tonight. She also looks surprised to see me. They both do actually.

'Shane,' I say, 'She wants you to leave.'

'Who the FUCK are you?' he says. 'Have you been *living* up there?'

'Yes… but-'

'You've been living in my attic? What the *FUCK*?' screams Harriet.

'It's not like that… I care about you Harriet…'

'How do you know my name? Are you some kind of pervert? What have you been doing?'

'Nothing. It's not like that…'

'You need to leave right now,' says Shane, pushing me towards the door, 'right now! I'm going to call the police!'

'Harriet…' I plead, trying to appeal to her. It doesn't work. Her beautiful face is filled with fear. It's the first time I've seen her in person. She looks nothing like I imagined from inside the ceiling. She's better.

Shane punches me in the face and I fall to the floor. I'm dazed but still conscious.

'Oh God Shane… help me…' says Harriet.

I don't give him the chance to strike me again. I'm out the door and on the run.

It's all gone wrong.

If I hadn't shifted my weight like that in the attic they never would have discovered me. She's so terrified now that she won't want to be alone tonight. Now Shane is going to win her back.

Fuck.

It's not fair.

'What are we doing here?' Lewis asked his friend.

Otto had a ridiculous grin on his face as he indicated at the space around them. He looked like a puppy, staring back with a look of optimism. Lewis surveyed the concrete corridor, waiting for an explanation that would never come.

'What am I looking at here?' he asked, more agitated this time. He liked Otto but he'd never heard a good idea come out of his mouth.

'Look at the corridor,' said Otto proudly, his stance displaying an unearned confidence that annoyed his colleague.

It was a service corridor, one that led away from their workplace and out into the larger CBD. Lewis was already familiar with it. Staff members often used it when they were walking to the train station and didn't want to get caught up in the elements. It was mostly made up of grey concrete blocks, with a lower than average ceiling.

'What about it?'

'The cameras!' said Otto pointing at the two security cameras above them. One was trained on each entrance.

'Just tell me what the *hell* you're talking about Otto. I don't have time for this.'

'Look! There's a blind spot between the cameras.'

He was right. While each of the static security cameras pointed at the doors there was an area between them that was not being recorded.

'So?'

'So we bring that goddamn security guard here and… rough her up!'

'Rough her up? Are you serious?'

'Yeah. Why not?'

'For starters she's a woman. I know she's built like a guy but she's still a woman. You want to fight a woman?'

'Well… together maybe.'

Lewis wondered why he'd been saddled with Otto. What horrible act had he committed in a past life that meant he required this much karmic correction?

'Are you an idiot? The cameras will still record you luring… I presume you'll be luring her… into the corridor. They'll see you walking in and out. Just because there's one area that isn't on camera doesn't mean that they won't know it's you!'

Otto threw his hands up in the air.

'Well I'm out of ideas mate! Bloody hell.'

The security guard in question was Bronwyn, a huge wall of intimidation that lacked empathy and had been harassing the boys for months. Unbelievably, it had all started over car parking.

The television station where they worked had an underground car park that was full of reserved spots. The news team, including its bevy of beautiful reporters, were each given a parking spot as a perk when they were hired. A majority of the spots were for the sales team and the executive level managers. The leftovers were allocated to the On Air shift workers, which included Otto and Lewis. The issue with parking arose during shift handover. All of the On Air staff had a half hour handover period to ensure someone was always monitoring the outgoing feeds. During this thirty-minute period there were twice as many On Air employees on station, meaning not enough car parks.

It was a problem that needed a solution. Everyone dealt with it differently. Some people decided to carpool to work, others took the train. It wasn't enough of course, and the issue remained.

The station was located in the Central Business District, and the surrounding parking options were considerably expensive. The On Air employees started parking in whatever vacant car parks they could, justifying that they would only be occupying them for thirty minutes at most. After that time someone would go home and they would move into their place. Bronwyn recognised their treachery almost right away and must have had nothing better to do but turn a molehill into a mountain.

She started by sending emails to all staff, demanding the offending employee move their car immediately. Then Bronwyn decided to patrol the underground parking lot during the handover period and put notes on the cars. She kept records of every license plate, for security reasons of course, and started a system of strikes. Bronwyn the parking queen threw her weight around and became a constant villain for the shift workers.

'Do you know what she did to Nora?' asked Otto when they were back in their seats.

'What?'

'Bronwyn disabled her work pass. So she couldn't leave through the gate,' Otto said with a shake of his head.

Lewis wasn't sure what to do. She was a menace and was certainly ruining an otherwise pleasant working environment. He decided to talk to his supervisor, as this could be quantified as a work issue that he thought was tantamount to bullying. Because they had all participated in a mandatory online course last year,

Lewis identified this as covert bullying because it was more secretive than overt bullying. His manager Esteban disagreed.

'We are assigned car parks by building maintenance and that's it,' said Esteban without an ounce of sympathy. He, of course, had his own car park on the third floor.

'But it's common sense,' said Lewis, 'can't you see that the changeover of staff is an issue? Can't we get permission to park *somewhere* for that thirty minutes?'

'I don't think there are any free spots to be honest. We've been assigned as many as possible.'

'Come on… you're letting Bronwyn get away with this.'

Esteban furrowed his brow.

'Is this really the hill you want to die on? *Parking spots* Lewis?'

'There is nowhere to park so we *have* to park in the empty bays. The news team aren't even there! They're off on location doing the news! Nobody is mad about this except for Bronwyn. I'll bet the news reporters don't even know its happening!'

Esteban finally agreed to look into it, which subdued Lewis. Unfortunately the building maintenance team completely misunderstood the request and did an audit of the entire car park. As a result they asked all of the heads of department how many parks they needed, leading to a reshuffle across the board. Somehow the On Air department, despite being on station at all times, managed to come out of the process with two fewer car parks.

It was incredibly frustrating for Lewis, who now experienced the fury of his peers on a daily basis. His work became a hostile environment. Only Otto, who was a simple creature, treated him the same.

Lewis had always been an unlucky employee. When he started work in regional television he was amazed to hear about the luxurious Christmas parties that were thrown every year, complete with thoughtful and expensive gifts. As a new employee he was forced to work the Christmas party that first year. And after an alcoholic incident resulted in a lawsuit the Christmas parties were significantly toned down. Management also cancelled the mid-year party as a cost cutting measure.

Lewis had been asked to chip in for many farewell presents over the years. The regional television channel had implemented a system where they looked at the amount raised by staff for a farewell gift and matched that amount. The system was abused shortly after Lewis arrived by a guy named Zane. He'd given hundreds of dollars to his girlfriend, who was also an employee at the station, and she'd put it in as a donation. They'd matched the amount and he'd laughed about it on his way out the door. They revoked the cash-based system in favour of a case-by-case basis.

When he was hired Lewis had learned that it took two years to be declared a senior employee, resulting in a nice pay rise. As he approached the two year mark management moved the goal posts and two years became three. His protests fell on deaf ears and he had to wait twelve months longer for his pay rise.

Lewis was also unlucky when he finally took the leap and moved from regional television to work at a Network level in the city. Nobody chipped in for his farewell present and his primary manager was sick on his last day. His final shift was extremely anti-climactic as a result, and he walked away from his role in regional TV empty handed.

Lewis thought that now, in the big city surrounded by his peers, metropolitan television would be different. He didn't want Bronwyn to ruin things for him here.

'I don't know what I can do. Telling Esteban only made things worse.'

'It's so petty.' Otto was always floating around and willing to lend an ear to Lewis' plight. 'And you're sure that you don't want to try my security camera idea?'

'No Otto… but keep thinking,' replied Lewis.

That Friday Lewis was late. He drove past the full car parks, shaking his head in frustration, and eventually gave up and put his vehicle in the parking structure across the street. When he walked into the building Bronwyn was filing her nails behind the security desk.

'No parks?' she asked casually without looking up.

'No…'

'That's a shame.' Bronwyn let a small smile creep onto her face. It was clear to Lewis that this was war.

When he finally got to his workstation the supervisor told him off.

'You're late again…'

'There were no car parks!' protested Lewis.

'I don't want to hear about it,' replied Esteban, 'just sit in for Barney. He's been waiting for a break.'

Lewis spoke softly so that Barney couldn't hear.

'Are you kidding me? Barney is always late back from his breaks. Are you going to have a go at him?'

'That's because he uses the bathroom a lot. It's not because he's late for his start time. Now hurry up… Barney has been snacking a lot today.'

The next night Lewis arrived to work even earlier in the hope that there would be at least one free spot. When there wasn't he called Esteban from the driver's seat.

'I'm here. I'm in the car park but there are no spots. Can you send someone home?' Lewis revved his idling car for emphasis.

'What?'

'I'm sitting in my car... send someone home so I can have their spot.'

'I can't do that. There are three people here that finish at the same time. How am I supposed to give one of them an early mark and ignore the other two?'

'Well... I'm here to work so I'll be out here until a spot opens up.'

His protest meant that Lewis was late yet again.

For his third shift Lewis took a taxi to work. When he arrived he asked the driver to wait, while he collected a cab charge voucher from reception. Bronwyn wasn't working and another security guard handed one over. His ride to work was charged to the TV station, a perk that was usually reserved for celebrities and On Air talent. When it was discovered Lewis was reprimanded yet again.

'I'm just trying to show you that this is a problem! A big problem Esteban!'

'I understand your frustration...' replied Esteban.

'You have your own spot! You don't understand it at all!'

Lewis was exasperated and sporting a vein that only appeared during his most agitated moments.

'I have to give you another warning. Don't take a taxi to work and if you do… don't charge it to the company.'

Lewis shook his head. Things became worse when he happened to see Bronwyn arriving for work one morning. He covertly watched as she parked, removing a duffel bag from the boot of her car. Lewis recognised the car she was parking in front of. It belonged to Tyrone, one of the other security guards. Bronwyn was executing exactly the same scam as Lewis had been accused of. She was parking her colleague in, only to swap cars later on after the shift handover. Bronwyn was able to get away with it because the parks weren't next to anything and Tyrone's car was able to manoeuvre away without her having to leave her post.

'I'm filthy about this,' he said explaining to Otto.

'What are you going to do?'

'She's beating the system… so I have to find a way to beat the system too.'

'But if you get another warning then they might fire you,' pleaded Otto, 'and I don't want to work here without you.'

'Nobody is getting fired.'

Lewis went out drinking with some of the reporters from the news team. He'd become chummy with them through various Christmas parties and team building exercises over the years. He was all set to explain his plight to them in person when from out of nowhere Joanna Marsh, the raven-haired reporter, kissed him. Being a hot-blooded man he kissed her right back, and the two went home together. They started a relationship and Lewis became the centre of a hive of office gossip.

'You're dating Joanna Marsh?' asked Esteban.

'Yeah. For about two weeks now.'

'*You?*'

'Yes.'

Sometimes Joanna drove him to work, which solved the parking situation for him, but it was only every now and then. Her job meant that she was up early and often on location filming stories for the evening news. Lewis made sure to ask her each and every time she would be away if he could use her parking spot on the third floor.

'Fine with me cutie,' she'd reply.

He felt powerful. Lewis held his head high knowing he had a reserved park at his disposal. Time passed happily and just as he'd finally forgotten about the parking lot war with Bronwyn she reignited it.

She was waiting for him on level three later that week.

'Is that your spot?' she demanded when Lewis stepped out of the car.

'No.'

'You can't park in other people's spots. You'll have to move,' stated Bronwyn.

'It's alright, I've asked and I can park here.'

'Oh you've *asked*? The parks in this section belong to news.'

'I know,' replied Lewis.

'Do you work in news now?'

'No.'

'This is Joanna Marsh's spot!'

'Yes Bronwyn I KNOW. I'm dating Joanna Marsh. She's my girlfriend and that's how I know this is her spot.'

Bronwyn paused for a moment.

'Well you'll have to move.'

'Why? She's out shooting a story. She's not coming back to the station. Why do you care?'

'I'm in charge of security here. There are rules and protocols that need to be followed.'

'Are you actually this petty? I know you park Tyrone in. You're doing exactly the same thing so you don't have to pay for parking across the road… it's fucking *three* hours minimum over there… do you do this because you have nothing else going on in your life? Are you that much of a *bitch*?'

'What did you just call me?'

'You heard me. Honestly… why don't you go and secure the front entrance? Who's guarding us now?'

Lewis walked away, not knowing whether retaliation would be swift or slow. While he was at his desk he wondered whether his car would be towed away. He'd heard that Bronwyn liked to do that but he'd never seen it himself. He wondered whether Esteban would approach, tapping him on the shoulder, and supply him with his third warning in as many months. Was he on the verge of being fired?

He walked past Bronwyn on his way out to his car holding his breath and expecting the worst. But it was sitting there on level three, untouched.

Perhaps there was nothing she could do. He considered that Bronwyn was probably watching him on the monitor so he tried to be confident. He got into his car, as if he'd always expected to see it there, and drove home.

There was an amazing sense of satisfaction for Lewis. He'd beaten Bronwyn at her own game. Sometimes he walked past the security desk with Joanna, whom Bronwyn seemed to have some respect for, and smiled to himself. She was as impotent as a defanged snake. It was an enjoyable couple of weeks for Lewis that he should have savoured.

Otto had heard rumours, but he was notoriously unreliable so Lewis didn't think anything of it at first. Then Esteban asked him to come in for a meeting.

'This is a difficult day,' he began, 'the company has decided that in order to reduce costs the On Air operations team will be moved overseas.'

'Overseas?'

'Yes,' continued Esteban, 'and the current operations will cease to exist.'

'So… what does that mean for me?'

'You're being made redundant. Everyone is.'

'Oh God.'

'I know.'

'When?' asked Lewis.

'The timeline on the project is flexible but it's looking like nine months. They've already started installing equipment.'

'Unbelievable… so what do you think you'll do?'

'Oh… I've been asked to move overseas and manage the newly formed department,' replied Esteban.

The department was dissolved within the year. It was like the entire On Air operation had been inside a giant metaphorical hourglass. From their position on the inside the sands were running down around them but it was impossible to know when the flow would stop entirely and their time would be up.

Joanna Marsh decided that Lewis wasn't for her and ended their relationship after the announcement. He could hardly blame her. Lewis had been so involved with his personal war against Bronwyn that he didn't see the signs. To add to the bitterness of the situation Bronwyn was also the guard tasked with walking Lewis out on his last day. The security staff were unaffected by the move, as the building they worked in had multiple tenants. Taking his security pass brought a gigantic grin to her face. Although Lewis had seemingly won the battle, Bronwyn had won the parking lot war between them.

DAISY

Harry Coleman surveyed the empty classroom from his high-back chair. The hum of the air conditioning unit was soothing and a welcome change from the cries of his teething daughter. Since his return to work Harry had found his home environment was no longer conducive for grading papers, a duty he'd previously been able to perform in the evening with a glass of whisky by his side. His daughter Lizzy required constant attention and while he'd abandoned his science fiction novel, he still needed to mark his student's history papers in order to keep his job. Harry liked working at Mornington College and being a part of the community. As a new father he felt tired but hopeful. He and Kelly had tried for many years to fall pregnant and now, in their late thirties, were thrilled about Lizzy's arrival. The first six months were a blur but their daughter was showing her personality now, and Kelly was talking about trying again.

'We probably wouldn't fall pregnant right away but we're not getting any younger. What do you think?' she'd suggested the night before.

Harry was feeling his age. He silently wished that they had been one of those couples that got pregnant straight away when they were twenty-two and now had a teenager. Everything seemed less manageable now at the age of thirty-eight. Incorporating little Lizzy into their marriage had been an adjustment and Harry wasn't certain he was capable of more change.

As he finished reading Trevor Simpson's paper on World War Two his mobile phone started to ring.

'Harry speaking.'

'Harry? It's Neil.'

Neil had been one of Harry's best friends growing up. While Harry had taken a post at Mornington College and moved away, Neil still lived in the small town where they'd grown up and had taken over the corner store. He often called his friend at the end of the day to fill him in on the town gossip. It was a strong friendship that had never been tested, with both men accepting the other completely.

'Neil? How are you mate?'

'I'm alright. How are *you* doing?'

Harry was confused by the question. He was the same as ever.

'I'm well. What's going on?' he asked.

'Oh… I thought you would have heard by now,' said Neil. Harry sensed the discomfort in his friend's voice.

'Heard what?'

'About Daisy. She died.'

For a moment Harry was sure he'd misheard Neil.

'What? Did you say Daisy… *died*?'

'I'm so sorry Harry.'

'I… how? How did she…?' The hum from the air conditioner now seemed noticeably louder.

'Car crash,' replied Neil flatly.

'That's awful.'

'I'm so sorry to be the one to tell you,' said Neil, 'I thought you might have seen it on Facebook or something.'

'No, I'm not on Facebook anymore… and I've been working,' replied Harry.

Social media had proven a distraction, and he'd had to report several disruptive students that had attempted to hack his personal account. It wasn't malicious as much as annoying.

'That's right. I forgot you're off of social media. I read that the funeral is in town on Saturday. Do you think you'll come back for it?'

'Um… I'm not sure. I'll have to talk to Kelly,' he said.

'Okay, fair enough. Listen sorry again. I feel terrible that I'm the one you had to hear it from. I know this must be hard.'

'It's alright Neil. Thank you for calling.'

'Alright, well let me know if you come back. I'll be around. We should get a beer,' he said, life returning to his voice.

Harry hung up the phone and sat back in a state of disbelief. He let the information sink in. Daisy – Harry's first love - had died in a car accident. He tried to remember the last time he'd seen her face. In person it had been almost eight years ago in a brief and slightly awkward chance meeting. During the past decade they had communicated twice a year to wish one another a happy birthday. Harry had enjoyed and looked forward to the emails initially, gleaning small fragments of Daisy's life from the paragraph or so of words. About three years ago the emails had stopped altogether. When her birthday came around Harry thought about continuing their correspondence but decided against it. If she didn't email him, he wouldn't bother her. She was probably happy in her life and had outgrown him. To hear that she had died was crushing. Harry wasn't looking forward to repeating the news out loud to Kelly that night. His wife had never understood his ongoing interest in Daisy and her life, which Harry put down to jealousy.

When he reported that the emails had stopped Kelly had struggled to hide her joy at the victory. Harry was worried that her reaction to his ex-girlfriend's death might be equally spirited.

Lizzy was mashing food between her fingers and cooing at the sensation. It was strange and wonderful to see the world through the eyes of a child. His wife Kelly had thick glasses that enhanced her green eyes to almost cartoonish proportions. She was sweet and doted on Lizzy's every need. Kelly never complained about waking up at two am with her daughter or about the tremendous amount of weight she had retained from the pregnancy. This was a secondary concern to Harry, who worried that another child might render his wife unrecognizable to him.

'Lizzy! Food goes in your mouth bubba,' said Kelly playfully to their daughter. She shot Harry a smile as if to say *isn't parenthood amazing?*

'What's wrong with you? You seem distracted,' said Kelly, her face transforming into a mask of concern.

'So I heard some bad news today.'

'What's going on?' she asked. Kelly had recently been concerned that he would lose his job somehow. He'd kept reassuring her that she was being irrational.

'Neil rang me at lunch and told me Daisy died.'

'Your ex-girlfriend Daisy?' asked Kelly, who was more surprised than shocked.

'Yeah.'

'Oh I'm sorry. She was still young.'

'Yeah about our age,' replied Harry. Daisy had died at thirty-seven, her next birthday would have been just after Christmas.

'What happened?'

'She was in a car accident apparently,' said Harry.

'Jesus.'

Lizzy broke the tension with a loud fart.

'Neil wanted to know if I was coming for the funeral.'

'Do you want to go?' He could sense his wife's hesitancy.

'I've been thinking that maybe I should.'

'When was the last time you spoke to her?' asked Kelly.

'Before we were married. Maybe eight or nine years ago.'

'I mean… if you *want* to go to…' she let her voice trail away. She couldn't pinpoint the feeling she was having. It felt as if her husband was *choosing* Daisy over her. He'd always held a special place in his heart for her, a place that Kelly could never touch.

'I think I would. I think… I'd like to say goodbye.'

Kelly hoped that this would be the last time he'd need to put Daisy first. Maybe this trip could offer him some closure.

'When is the funeral?' asked Kelly.

'On the weekend.'

'I can't go this weekend. My mother's group is having that bake sale for ovarian cancer.'

'I just thought… I would go by myself actually.'

'Oh. Alright.'

'It's just that I think I won't be there long. Just the weekend really. And I'll probably have some drinks with Neil and catch up,' said Harry, fumbling through the list of reasons he wanted to be alone. Kelly didn't know Daisy. He didn't want to attend the funeral with her and a crying Lizzy, although it would be the most appropriate place for their often-bawling daughter.

'That's a much better idea actually. You know, Lizzy's probably a bit too young to go on a plane anyway,' said Kelly.

'And I'm not really technically *invited*… I mean they might not be expecting me there. I'd just be showing up to pay my respects.'

'How do you know where it is?'

'It's all on Facebook. Neil emailed me the link,' said Harry.

'Right, sounds like a plan. And maybe you should get back on Facebook like I've been suggesting. Then I can tag you in the pictures of Lizzy that I post.'

That night Harry bathed Lizzy, delighting in her feverish splashing. He purchased a plane ticket and set aside a bag for the trip. In bed Kelly threw herself at her husband but he wasn't in the mood. His head was full of memories and if they made love it wouldn't be fair to his wife. He would have been imagining Daisy in her prime.

The airport wasn't busy that Friday morning. Harry had opted out of work citing a death, but keeping the details vague. The fact that he had to travel interstate for a funeral had sealed it, and the Principal had allowed him the day off. Kelly had insisted on driving him and now stood impatiently waiting for his flight to be called. It was a relief for Harry when he finally heard the announcement.

'That's me then,' he said giving his wife a hug.

'Call us when you land?' she asked, holding up Lizzy like a prop.

'I will. Bye-bye Lizzy. Daddy will see you soon,' he said kissing his daughter on the forehead.

She flinched against his light stubble before dribbling aimlessly.

'I love you,' said Kelly.

'I love you too.'

It had been a while since Harry had been on a plane but the protocol seemed the same. He was still too tall to comfortably sit for long flights and had already decided he'd need to stand, stretching at regular intervals. He'd managed to get a seat in the exit row adjacent to a woman approaching her sixties, defying her aging hair with a bright red dye. As take-off became imminent an Air Hostess approached them.

'Sir, are you aware you are seated in the emergency exit row?' she asked Harry, flashing him an impossibly white smile.

'Yes.'

'So in the event of an emergency do you feel comfortable assisting with an evacuation?'

'Of course,' he replied. He hoped the duty would only be a ceremonious one, as in the event of an emergency Harry had no idea what he would be capable of.

'Please have a read of this.'

She handed him a laminated card and walked away, prompting the red-haired woman to speak.

'Do you fly much?' she asked.

'No not really,' he confessed.

'I like it. I fly as often as I can. I have grandchildren all over so I make excuses to go and see them.'

'That's nice. I'm sure they appreciate it.'

She indicated toward Harry's ring.

'I see you're married.'

'Yes I am.'

'Do you have any kids?'

'Yes, just the one. A little girl,' replied Harry.

'What's her name?'

'Lizzy. Elizabeth.'

'Lovely. Any photos?'

'Um… yeah, sure.'

He pulled out his phone and shared his favourite recent picture of his daughter. The still portrayed Lizzy giggling at a series of funny faces he'd pulled.

'Oh how lovely,' said the woman, smiling at the image. 'Are you going to have more?'

'We'll have to see how we go.'

'Kids make you live longer. They're the best thing for the soul.'

'Is that right?' asked Harry, suddenly feeling like rejecting the duties of a man in the emergency row and swapping seats with anyone who would care to.

'I can tell you're a good father. Now if you want to be a good husband give your wife another baby!'

The motel room was close to the airport and very standard discount fare. The TV Remote was attached to the unit with an unbreakable metal tether, rendering it useless should the occupant desire the ability to change channels from more than fifty centimetres away. He'd parked his bag at the foot of the bed, deciding against unpacking anything right away. Harry hung his black suit up, encased in a protective carry bag, knowing that it was the only item he really needed for the trip. He called his wife, who had tried to reach him seven times during the flight.

'Hi honey. Just checked into the motel.'

'That's nice Harry, listen I've just found something out. I'm pregnant!' she squealed over the phone.

'What do you mean?'

'I couldn't wait to tell you. I did a test before I took you to the airport and it was negative so I threw it in the bin but then when I saw it again it was positive.'

'Wow.'

Harry suddenly felt extremely irresponsible.

'It's amazing isn't it? I always wanted our kids to be born close together. I thought we would have more difficulty but I guess we're just lucky!'

'That's great. I'm speechless.'

'I knew you'd be happy. Let's have a dinner out when you're back to celebrate.'

'Okay Kel.'

Harry wanted to end the call but Kelly wasn't done.

'Do you think we'll have a boy or a girl this time? Shall we make it a surprise?'

'I hate surprises.'

'Oh no you don't! Well we can talk about everything when you're back.'

'Sounds good.'

'Enjoy your night. And good luck tomorrow.'

'Okay, I'll tell you about it later.'

'Okay… bye… oh wait! Here's Lizzy, she's awake now!'

There was a rustling and Harry sensed he was now on speakerphone.

'Hi Lizzy-boo,' he said.

There was more fumbling before his wife spoke.

'Sorry, she's trying to put the phone in her mouth.'

'Never mind.'

That night Harry overindulged on Chinese food and dreamt about Daisy. He imagined her with a huge pregnant belly and woke up in a sweat.

The funeral had started earlier than expected. There was a gathering of mourners heaped together underneath a tree, trying to avoid the penetrating rays of sun. A shiny black coffin lay in the open absorbing heat. The forty or so people in attendance were all dressed appropriately in black with the exception of Daisy's father who wore a white blazer.

Harry recognised him right away. Here was a man that he'd feared in his youth. When Harry was with Daisy her father Mitchell had put him through his paces. He'd forced Harry to play trivial pursuit and then openly mocked his lack of knowledge. He was also a former boxer and maintained a rigorous routine to stay in shape. Mitchell would recruit him for a run and then marvel at his lack of stamina. There was always a feeling that Harry wasn't good enough for Daisy. The seeds of that idea had festered longer than Harry was proud to admit. Here and now at her funeral Mitchell seemed smaller somehow. Harry had no need to win his affections and found for the first time a sense of ease in his presence.

Daisy's mother Linda was on her knees. Nobody touched her or offered to help her up, seemingly it was understood that this was how she wanted to grieve for her eldest child. Perhaps sitting down in the sun made her feel closer to Daisy. She did not cry but stared at the coffin.

Harry lingered to one side of the procession. He was too far away to hear the prayers and readings from the minister. It was important for him to be there. He needed this moment to say goodbye, telling himself he'd wander over to her grave later by himself. He was glad to see such a turnout. It verified what he already knew: Daisy was loved by all.

The casket was finally lowered into the earth while some generic string music played. Harry thought she would have hated the music. Daisy had always been particular about playlists. Harry associated so many songs with moments they'd shared. As people started to scamper away he sensed a presence approaching to his left. When Harry turned he found himself facing the sun. With only a partial view of the woman beside him he thought his eyes were playing tricks on him. He thought he saw Daisy.

'Hi Harry.'

It was impossible.

'Daisy?'

'No, it's me Maggie.'

Daisy's younger sister had grown up and was the spitting image of Daisy. Harry was flabbergasted. Maggie actually resembled his ex-girlfriend during the period they had dated, right down to the black fedora on her head.

'Jesus… *Maggie*? You look so much like… you've grown up,' he stammered.

'Thanks. You too I guess.'

'How long has it been?' asked Harry.

'About fifteen years I think. Can't say I've been keeping track,' she said with the same familiar smile as her sister.

'Wow.'

'Yeah,' replied Maggie.

'You look so different.'

'Well, it's been a long time.'

During his relationship with Daisy he'd tolerated Maggie. As an inquisitive teenager she'd wanted to hang around with them, but a combination of hormones and opportunity meant they discarded her often.

'I'm so sorry about your sister.'

'Thank you. And thanks for coming,' said Maggie.

'Yeah, I only just heard.'

'I wondered if you'd show up.'

'I hope you don't mind that I did?' enquired Harry.

'It's a lovely gesture I think.'

'How are your parents doing?' he asked, spotting them in the distance.

'They're okay. I keep telling them that it's not so bad – they almost lost both of us – but I'm still here.'

'You were in the car too?' This was a revelation.

'Yeah. Daisy was driving.'

'I'm so sorry. That must have been horrible.'

'It's a weird way to find out you aren't the favourite child. I'm not sure they would be as broken up if the situation were reversed.'

Her candid comments startled Harry.

'I'm sure they're just grieving. I'm glad you're ok.'

'Thanks. Are you coming to the wake?'

He hadn't considered imposing on their private gathering.

'Oh no. I probably shouldn't. I wasn't really invited to this.'

Suddenly Maggie turned and shouted out to her parents. It felt very odd to see someone shouting at a funeral. They walked over slowly and Maggie became impatient, calling out to them as they walked.

'Mum! Dad! Look who I've found!' she called, pointing at Harry. He felt extremely uncomfortable again.

Mitchell and Linda strode over arm in arm. After he recognised Harry, Mitchell threw his arm around him and gave him a hug. When he stepped back Linda gave a small wave, as if she was brimming with emotion and didn't want to set herself off with any grand gesture.

'Harry. Thanks for coming,' said Mitchell.

'Hello Mr. Pope. Mrs. Pope. I'm so sorry for your loss,' he replied and bowed his head a little.

'Thank you,' said Mitchell.

'I was just telling Harry that he should come to the wake,' chimed in Maggie.

'No… I don't mean to intrude. I just came to pay my respects to Daisy,' said Harry quickly.

'Nonsense. You were a major part of my daughter's life. You should come,' said Mitchell.

'You're very kind but I-'

'I insist,' said Mitchell, cutting him off. 'Do you still remember where we live?'

'Yes I do.'

'We will see you at the house then,' said Mitchell, who didn't wait for a reply as he and Linda started to walk away.

'Where's your car?' asked Maggie.

'I took a taxi,' replied Harry.

'C'mon. It's only a short walk.'

Maggie led Harry away from the cemetery and they walked side by side toward a concrete path. The day had become more tolerable, the sun now hiding away behind a pack of clouds. Harry put his hands in his pockets and tried not to scuff his best black shoes.

'So did you ever get married?' asked Maggie.

'I did.'

'Congratulations.'

'Thanks.'

'Who's the lucky lady?' she asked, giving Harry a nudge with her elbow.

'Kelly. We met online.'

'Wow. Weren't you worried she would turn out to be a fifty-year old man or something?'

'It never occurred to me. She was actually the first and last person I ever decided to meet. So I guess I never had a bad experience with online dating,' he replied with a smile.

'And then you deleted your dating app and never looked back?'

'Yeah, more or less.'

'Well isn't that romantic. I always thought you and Daisy might end up together,' confessed Maggie, still facing forward.

'Yeah, I know what you mean.'

'She never really got serious with anyone after you, you know?'

'She didn't?'

It was in that moment he wished they'd emailed more often, or that they had stayed friends on Facebook or something. He knew so little about her life in the lead up to her death.

'No. You might have been her soul mate.'

'Maybe.'

'But now you have Kelly,' stated Maggie.

'Yeah.'

They walked on in silence for a little while across a main road and past several old restaurants. They were not the same establishments he remembered. There was also a wall covered in graffiti, which had been partially scrubbed clean.

'Why did you two break up by the way?' asked Maggie as they passed the post office.

'Oh I don't know if we should talk about this,' he replied.

'Okay… doesn't matter. We're here.'

The door to the Pope family home was just around the corner. They'd always lived within walking distance to the shops, which was how Daisy and Harry had met. In what felt like a past life Harry had worked as a cashier in the corner store that Neil now ran. Daisy had made sure to visit him regularly back then. Though they saw each other at school it was easier to bond that way. Daisy had seemed unapproachable surrounded by friends on the playground but in the shop he could get through to her. It was the beginning of their story. When they reached the wake there were cars parked everywhere. Harry hadn't counted on seeing so many of Daisy's relatives but they seemed to flock to him, sharing stories and giving him condolences that he didn't know what to do with. Maggie stood right beside him, taking things in her stride.

'It was a beautiful service,' one woman said on her way out the door.

'Thank you for saying so,' replied Maggie. 'And thank you for coming.'

'I'm so glad you were alright… after the accident,' another said.

'Thank you. Me too,' she replied.

Soon the bulk of people had left and Harry found himself alone with the Pope family. Linda made him a cup of tea and they sat down at the dining table. It felt a little bit like an interrogation.

'So what can you tell us about your life in Sydney?' asked Linda.

'Well I'm a history teacher now and at the moment I'm working as a tutor and part-time librarian.'

'And you like that type of work?' she asked.

'Yes I'm enjoying it so far,' replied Harry, shifting in his seat.

'And what does your wife do?' asked Maggie.

'Oh I didn't know you were married,' added Mitchell.

'Yeah it's been a few years now. She isn't working at the moment,' said Harry.

'Is she looking for work or…' Linda asked, letting her voice trail off.

'No, she's actually just told me that she's pregnant.'

'Wow. Congratulations,' said Linda.

'I probably shouldn't have said anything. It's really early,' he added quickly. It was weighing on his mind.

'That's exciting,' said Mitchell.

'Oh good for you,' chimed in Linda.

'Thanks.'

Harry felt strange receiving congratulations on the day that his ex-girlfriend was being buried.

'I always wanted more kids,' said Linda with a faraway look in her eye.

'I always wanted less,' said Mitchell.

There was an awkward silence as Mitchell realised his faux pas.

'That is to say, two kids was a handful,' he added.

'Yes I expect it will be,' replied Harry.

'And so you already have a baby, is that right?'

'Yes, Lizzy's almost ten months old now. It's flying by.'

'That's going to be an uphill battle. Two kids under two,' said Mitchell.

'Try to sleep when the babies sleep,' added Linda.

'I'm sure we'll do that.'

'It's really so good of you to come Harry. I wondered what had become of you after all this time,' said Linda collecting some empty cups and taking them to the kitchen.

'Yes, I definitely fell off the grid a little.'

'It's nice to see you got married and settled down though. You know I always compared Daisy's boyfriends to you,' said Mitchell.

This was a pleasant surprise to Harry. Perhaps Mitchell liked him after all.

'Oh is that right?' asked Harry, dying for more details.

'Yeah,' said Mitchell, 'there were a few tossers that I didn't like at all. They had the common sense to stay away today.'

'But we're glad *you* came,' said Linda quickly.

'Thank you. I thought I should,' he replied.

Harry excused himself and retreated to the bathroom. There he was shocked to find that the ensuite had undergone a renovation since he'd been there last. There were now two showerheads instead of one. They were side by side, allowing Daisy's parents to wash their bodies simultaneously. At least, that's what Harry *hoped* they were installed for.

He returned to the group, but couldn't look them in the eye.

'I'm tired now. I'm going to have an early night,' said Linda excusing herself.

'Yes, I should be leaving too,' said Harry as he stood up. He was happy to go.

Mitchell shook Harry's hand and they left the room together. Maggie smiled and rolled down her sleeves.

'I can drop you somewhere if you like?' she offered.

'It's fine, I can just take a taxi,' he said.

'Come on, you're doing me a favour. I don't really want to be here right now.'

In was an intense day and Harry could understand Maggie's mindset. He accepted the ride and soon they were on their way towards the airport motel. With the wind whipping Maggie's hair around Harry felt like he was twenty years old again. He'd often taken road trips with Daisy where they'd stayed in dingy places together. She'd often highlighted that the worst trips were the most memorable. Daisy had been right. Harry never forgot the leaky tap that went all night or the tree that almost fell on her car. He could sense her even though she was gone.

'So is this your car?' he asked Maggie.

'No it's Mum's. I don't own a car. I used to borrow Daisy's but obviously I can't do that anymore,' she replied.

'It must have been a horrible experience for you,' he said.

'Not really. I was knocked out on impact and unconscious. I woke up and Daisy was already dead. It sort of feels like a dream actually. I keep expecting her to walk through the door,' replied Maggie.

'I know what you mean. It sort of feels like she's still here.'

'Yeah. I feel her too,' said Maggie with a nod.

'You really do look so much like her, you know?'

'Do I?'

'It's like seeing a ghost,' said Harry.

'That must be strange for you.'

'It's odd, yes.'

Harry stared straight ahead.

'Are you excited about becoming a father again?' she asked.

'No. In twelve years I'll be fifty. I'm too old,' he said.

'You'll be fine.'

When they reached the motel Maggie parked and turned off the car engine.

'What a shithole,' she said with a laugh.

'It really is.'

'If it looks like this on the outside how bad is it inside?' she asked.

'Bad,' he replied. 'The shower has a raised plastic tub at the base that you have to step into… maybe to like create a bath for a kid… and I slept so badly last night because of this main road.'

'They should just knock this motel down,' she said.

'Or burn it to the ground,' he added.

'Are you going to invite me in for a drink? I brought whisky,' said Maggie, revealing a bottle in the glove compartment.

Harry wanted to say yes. The last time he'd indulged in drink was when he could grade papers at home, just before Lizzy was born.

'Yeah come on in.'

When Maggie saw the inside of the room she cackled loudly.

'It's so much worse than I could have imagined!'

'It was last minute!' he replied, trying to justify his choice.

His mobile phone rang.

'You going to get that?' asked Maggie.

'Yeah… it's Kelly.'

Harry answered the call and turned to face away from Maggie.

'Hi hon,' he started, 'how are you?'

'Good. How was the service?'

'Fine.'

'That's good. So you're coming home tomorrow?' asked Kelly.

'Yeah I'll be back around lunchtime.'

'Do you want me to pick you up?'

'No… I'll just get the bus. I'll see you when I get back,' he said.

'What are you doing tonight?'

'Tonight?' he asked, and turned around to face Maggie. She raised her eyebrows, sharing his curiosity. 'I might get a drink with Neil.'

They said their farewells and Harry hung up the phone.

'Are you going to see Neil?' asked Maggie.

'Probably not. I don't think I have it in me,' he replied.

'So you just lied to your wife?'

'Yeah.'

'Why?'

'She was always kind of jealous of Daisy… what with her being my first love. I just don't want… I guess… Kelly just doesn't understand.'

'But she knows Daisy's dead, right? She can't be jealous anymore.'

'It's irrational but I think she is. I'm a different person now. She never knew me when I lived here and she doesn't want me to regress into the guy I was back then.'

'Why? I always liked that guy,' said Maggie.

'You did?'

'Yeah. I always wanted to hang out with you and Daisy because I liked you. You say that Daisy was your first love? Well you were kind of mine.'

'Wow.'

'I mean… I was basically invisible to you. I was just a kid. You were with my sister…'

'I had no idea,' he replied.

Maggie took a swig from the bottle and offered it to Harry. He took a slug and set the bottle down.

'Maggie, I-'

She moved quickly, grabbing onto Harry as if she might fall down without the support of his body. She pressed her lips against his and the two lingered in a silent embrace. The rest just unfolded organically. Their bodies fit together easily and they made love that night. At times Harry thought of Daisy, which he forgave himself for. Maggie didn't speak, which added to the spell he was under. When it was over they lay down and Harry started to cry.

'Are you alright?' she asked.

'I haven't cried about Daisy… until now.'

'Oh that's fine… I thought you were crying because of me… because of what we did.'

'No. It's not about us.'

'Did you say *us*?' asked Maggie.

'Do you want there to be an *us*?' he asked quickly.

'I've always wondered what it would like to be with you. This was unfinished business. This was grief. Now neither of us has to wonder.'

'You don't want to see if there's something here? You don't feel like this could be a second chance?'

'Go home to your wife Harry. I'm glad we did this but I think I should leave.'

Maggie got dressed, kissed him goodbye and the two walked out to Linda's car.

'You want to know why we broke up?' he asked.

'Yes.'

'We lost a child. Daisy was pregnant and the baby didn't survive. Things were different after that and she ended it with me. I didn't pursue her… I didn't fight to get her back. I was young and I thought I'd have more time. And now she's gone.'

'She's still around. I can feel her,' said Maggie with a smile. She reached into her purse and found a printed photograph, which she handed to Harry.

'Is that Daisy?' he asked.

'Yeah. It was taken earlier this year.'

In the photograph Daisy was smiling and holding a portable coffee mug in one hand. Harry thought she looked more beautiful than ever.

'You can keep that. Goodbye Harry.'

'Thanks Maggie. Take care.'

The next morning Harry was at the airport bright and early. The one good thing about the motel was that it was basically walking distance to the terminal, meaning he now had time on his hands. Harry decided to call Neil and apologise for not seeing him during his visit.

'That's okay mate, next time, yeah?' said Neil.

'It's just that… going to the funeral really did a number on me. It's been such a strange weekend.'

'I completely get it. It's hard to say goodbye.'

'I've been feeling like I probably should have married Daisy, right? I mean I know we were dumb kids but I was happy. I should have stayed here and we should have been together.'

'You're always going to have regrets Harry. It's natural,' replied Neil.

'Did I make a mistake?'

'Maybe. But it's too late now.'

'I know.'

'You love Kelly though, right?' asked his friend.

'Sure.'

'Well then let me put it to you this way… I've never been in love. The way I see it you've had two chances at it. Put that into perspective… you've been spoilt really. Go home to your loving wife and appreciate what you've got,' said Neil.

'You're right. Thanks mate.'

'Hang in there buddy. I'll call you soon.'

The only available seat back to Sydney was an aisle and Harry found himself quite comfortable this time. He didn't think the dimensions of the seat were any different to the first flight but somehow he fit better into the space. On his left was a woman in her forties wearing a turtleneck. He smiled politely at her.

'Hi there,' he said.

'Hi.'

'Going home to Sydney?' Harry asked.

'Yeah back to see my family,' the woman replied.

'Me too. Home to the wife.'

'That's nice.'

'Did you want to see a picture?' asked Harry.

'Ah… sure…' replied the woman hesitantly.

He reached into his breast pocket and pulled out the picture of Daisy.

'That's my wife.'

The stranger looked at the image and gave him a polite smile.

'She's beautiful.'

'She really is,' he replied, welling up.

Harry dried his eyes as inconspicuously as he could and returned the picture to the pocket closest to his heart.

CAN I BUY YOU A DRINK?

In the bathroom Porter had seen at least three flies. There might have been more but he didn't want to stay and count them in such vile surroundings. He imagined the flies had landed on the backs of sweaty patrons who had transported them into the stalls. Maybe in time they would find a customer on the way out and hitch a ride back towards the bar. They were pests, and Porter made sure the bathroom door closed tightly behind him when he was done.

After his third whisky he realised that his hand was now sticking to the ring-stained bar. Had he spilled that much? Porter didn't think it was possible. He was drunker than he ought to be, and so he embraced the grimy surface with his forearm. It didn't seem to matter now. Porter was savouring every drop of this precious liquid tonight. At twelve dollars a glass he couldn't afford to waste it. Upon closer inspection the glasses themselves weren't particularly clean. Was anything in the joint hygienic? Probably not. Perhaps the bartender, busy flirting with the two blondes seated at the bar, had forgotten how to do his job.

The best feature of the establishment was its karaoke machine, which had somehow been stocked with songs from this decade. It attracted a female demographic, which on any other night would appeal to Porter. Tonight he found the idea of talking to the opposite sex a hassle. He'd left his girlfriend, who he'd dubbed *Cupcake* because of her job as a pastry chef, alone for the weekend and the results had been a disaster. In a moment of carnal weakness she'd slept with her ex-boyfriend, a man they'd previously dubbed *Fuckstick*. To make matters worse Cupcake had engaged in the activity in the backseat of *his* car, which she was borrowing so she could get to work.

Cupcake had gotten to work alright.

What was it about Fuckstick that made her backslide into his arms like that? She was a rotten liar and the affair was written all over her face. Why had she hurt him like that?

He ordered another drink and noticed a man at the jukebox staring at him. He was older, with salt and pepper hair and a cardigan. The man nodded at Porter and, probably due to common courtesy, he found himself nodding back politely. The man approached.

'Can I buy you a drink?' he asked.

'Sure.'

'What will it be?'

'Whisky. Thanks.'

The bartender was quick with the drinks this time.

'I'm Bevan,' said the man.

'Porter. Thanks for the drink.' He took a deep sip.

'What's brought you here tonight?' asked Bevan, before indulging in a drink of his own.

'A rotten woman.'

'Ain't they all rotten?' he said with a laugh.

'Been around the block a few times, have you?' asked Porter. 'You tell me.'

'Women are only looking out for themselves, that's for sure. They settle down with a man for shelter. Women are primitive… *primal* beasts at the core. They'll have your children because they want to get their hooks into you. I'll never trust a woman again,' replied Bevan.

'I wish I'd known that a week ago. Maybe I wouldn't be drowning my sorrows now.'

'What's her name?'

'Cupcake.'

'Funny name.'

Porter told Bevan about her job at the bakery.

'The nickname's fitting then. What's she done wrong?'

'She had sex with her Fuckstick ex-boyfriend.'

'Shit.'

'In my car.'

'Bartender!' Bevan called, standing up, 'we're going to need two more drinks.'

'I appreciate that.' The alcohol had taken an even deeper hold.

'Women are the worst. But the good thing is there are plenty of them.'

'I guess so.'

'See we're primal beasts too,' said Bevan, 'and we only want one thing.'

'Sex.'

'Naturally. So you can't blame Fuckstick really. He was just being a man.'

'It takes two to tango,' Porter replied.

'Yeah… but she could have danced alone. She made the call. She fucked the Fuckstick.'

'True. So what brings you here tonight? The jukebox?' asked Porter.

'I was a musician once… in another life,' replied Bevan.

'And now?'

'Now that seems like a memory.'

'But isn't music kind of like riding a bike? Muscle memory, right?' asked Porter.

'I suppose it might be. I'm not game to find out.'

'Why not?'

'I gave it up when my wife died. She was a composer and she used to make beautiful music.'

'I'm sorry for your loss.'

Porter waved down the bartender and bought them both another drink.

'Thanks,' said Bevan.

'So why did you give it up? Not to be rude but I would think that playing her music would honour her memory.'

'There was another composer that was working with her on the music. At the end… when she passed away… he stole everything they'd worked on together. He took sole ownership of it and there was nothing I could do. I couldn't prove what she'd done.'

'That's shit.'

'Yeah… it put a sour taste in my mouth. Ruined music for me I suppose.'

'Well maybe one day you'll pick up… sorry… what did you play?' asked Porter.

'The violin.'

'Well maybe you'll pick up the violin again one day.'

'I don't think so.'

'Have you found a better hobby then?'

'Besides drinking you mean?' replied Bevan with a chuckle.

'It's an easy one to fall back on.'

The two men sat silently for a moment as they drank, and took in their surroundings. The jukebox was the loudest thing in the room. A group of women decided to dance to a country song that neither of the men recognised. The bartender finally dragged a wet rag past the two and they both picked up their glasses in unison.

'So what's next for you and Cupcake?' asked Bevan. 'You want her dead?'

'That would be a lot easier than fighting with her.'

'My wife and I met later in life,' said Bevan. 'I wish I'd had more years to fight with her.'

'I'll bet your wife never fucked around on you though.'

'No… I'll give you that one. She was loyal. We understood each other.'

'So… forgive me for asking this… but didn't you say all women were… primal beasts just looking for someone rich to sponge off?' asked Porter.

'They sure are.'

'And so your wife was the last good one?'

'No… she was as beastly as they come. But she and I both knew what we were getting ourselves into. Plus the sex was worth all the trouble.'

Porter chuckled and finished his drink. Bevan still had a full glass of whisky in front of him.

'So I guess you have to ask yourself… are the *cupcakes* that good?'

'Not if I have to share them.'

'Where is this bakery she works at?' asked Bevan.

Porter told him.

'I've never been there before,' he replied.

Porter gave him some loose directions.

'Oh yeah… that's not too far away.'

'I know,' said Porter, as he checked his watch. 'Cupcake will be up soon. That's probably the worst part about dating a baker. Their sleep schedule sucks.'

'My wife used to be an early riser too. I used to enjoy waking up in bed alone, knowing she'd be in the kitchen or the study. Now I hate it.'

'Have you ever thought about doing something about that guy that stole her music?' asked Porter.

'I think about him often actually. If I can track him down… I'll do something… maybe.'

Bevan stood up and placed a hand on Porter's shoulder.

'Well… good luck finding him.'

'Thanks. You should have this one,' said Bevan, indicating to the untouched glass on the bar. 'I'm not going to need it.'

'Great. Cheers.'

'Do you think you'll be here a while?' asked Bevan. 'You're not going to see Cupcake before work?'

'No… I might just stay here. Avoid her completely.'

'Probably for the best,' said Bevan with a nod. 'It was nice meeting you properly.'

'Yeah… nice meeting you too.'

Bevan brushed his hands against the front of his pants and left the bar.

Porter stirred the glass of whisky with his finger before drinking it. How had things gotten so bad with Cupcake? The important question now was whether or not he wanted to be with her, and whether or not Fuckstick was out of the picture. If she could be loyal, then it was worthwhile to Porter. Was Bevan right though? Were women untrustworthy? He looked up and noticed a female bartender had just started her shift.

'Hey!' he called, getting her attention.

'Hey. Can I get you something?' she replied. She wore a black singlet, presumably the required uniform, and had her jet-black hair tied up in a ponytail.

'Can I ask you something?'

'You just did.'

'No, I mean can I ask you something else?'

'Yeah… you just did again.'

'I want to know if you think all women are… *beasts*?'

'What?' she replied, her tone defensive.

'Do you think that men can trust women? I mean… is that a good idea?' asked Porter.

'Are you drunk? Should I cut you off?'

'No…' Porter was definitely drunk but tried his best to hide it.

'Can men trust women? Is that what you want to know?' asked the barmaid. 'Well let me ask you this: Can *women* trust men?'

'Yeah… I see what you're getting at. We're all untrustworthy,' said Porter, flicking the ice at the bottom of his glass.

'If a woman says she'll do something, it gets done. I can't say the same about men,' stated the bartender.

'Will you get me another whisky?' asked Porter.

'I will… but it's going to be your last for the night.'

'Ok.'

She turned around and fixed his drink.

'See what I mean? I said I'd do something and it got done.'

'Maybe you're one of the good ones.'

'Yeah, maybe. It sounds like you got hurt by one of the bad ones. Is that right?'

'Hurt is an understatement.'

'Well, hurt heals. You'll love again.'

'Yeah? Sounds like you know something about it.'

'I do, but I don't feel the need to tell strangers about it,' she replied sharply.

Porter wondered if he had over-shared with Bevan, but decided that it was a mutually enjoyable exchange. Suddenly, and without really thinking Porter found himself staring at the bartender's breasts. He was caught immediately.

'Seems like you might want to tip me,' she said.

'Yeah I might.'

'With cash I hope.'

Porter took a twenty from his wallet and gave it to the woman. He would have preferred to take her home and sleep with her but she'd tolerated him enough to earn the money.

'Now why don't you get yourself home. It's Tuesday. Plenty of week left. Call you a cab?'

Defeated, Porter nodded.

The bartender smiled and walked away. He checked his watch again. Cupcake would be on her way to work now. It was probably safe to head home and sleep it off.

The taxi took too long and drove too slowly for his liking. When the driveway was in sight he breathed a sigh of relief. Cupcake had taken his tainted car to work. Porter could have a sleep and fight with her later. He threw some money at the driver and went inside. He collided with his pillow and passed out.

It was late afternoon when Porter came to. His mouth was dry so he rolled out of bed and headed for the kitchen sink. He drank in big gulps straight from the tap.

He'd missed several calls during the morning but none of them were from Cupcake. She was probably with Fuckstick.

There was a confrontation brewing if that were the case. And Porter needed his car back. His head was throbbing. He grabbed two chewable vitamin C tablets and collapsed on the sofa. The knock on the door that followed seemed frantic.

'Are you Porter?' asked the tall and weathered man. He wore a suit and looked at least sixty-five. His head seemed squared off, with his grey hair fashioned into a flat top.

'Yeah that's me.'

He asked about Cupcake.

'She's my girlfriend.'

He asked if Porter knew where she was.

'She went to work this morning. I don't know where she is now.'

He asked if they'd been together the night before.

'Who are you?' asked Porter.

'My name is Wilkins. I'm a Police Officer.'

'Has something happened?'

'I'm sorry to report that your girlfriend was found dead this morning in a vehicle that's registered to you.'

'What?'

Porter's face froze. Wilkins studied it for clues.

'It appears that someone tried to hijack your vehicle. She might have resisted and after a struggle she was struck with a blunt instrument. We are still trying to find the murder weapon,' said Wilkins flatly.

'I… I can't believe this.'

'Yes… we are theorising that the assailant then fled the scene. I realise that this is a lot to take in but as it's your car, and your girlfriend, I need to eliminate you as a suspect.'

'I was out drinking.'

'Where?'

Porter told him about the bar.

'And you were there at what time?'

Porter told the officer to the best of his ability.

'Ok… I'll need to check the surveillance tapes and confirm your alibi. There is one more thing.'

'Yeah?'

'I haven't been able to reach the parents of the deceased. Would you be willing to identify the body?'

Porter needed to see her corpse. It was the only way he'd know for sure.

'Um… I *guess* I could. I'd need a ride.'

'I'd be happy to take you. If you could just put on some pants we can go.'

Wilkins and Porter shared an uncomfortable drive to the station. Porter kept thinking about Cupcake. He refused to believe she was dead. Wilkins systematically looked at Porter, checking for signs of guilt. He refused to believe this man was innocent. He needed to check the surveillance tapes. It was the only way he'd know for sure.

It was definitely Cupcake.

The right side of her face was frozen in fear. She looked pale against the white sheet. Wilkins unveiled the left side of Cupcake's face. Her skull was caved in and no effort had been made to clean her up. Porter walked straight out of the room, wishing that he'd never seen her like that. Wilkins followed, a curious look forming on his face. Porter felt dizzy. Cupcake didn't deserve this.

'So can you confirm the identity of the deceased?' asked Wilkins.

'Yes. It's her.'

'I'm sorry for your loss. This is never easy.'

Porter wanted to cry but he was in shock. Wilkins dropped him home and gave him the number of a local funeral parlour.

'Can I count on you to call her parents?' he asked.

'They've always hated me,' started Porter, 'I don't think they'd want to hear this from me.'

'That's fine. We can arrange for someone else to tell them.'

'Thanks.'

'If you need anything… or remember anything that might be helpful please give me a call,' said Wilkins as he offered his card to Porter.

'I will.'

Wilkins was in touch again later that day to confirm Porter's alibi.

'The gentleman you're drinking with in this video, how well do you know him?' he asked.

'I met him that night. We had a drink and that was it.'

'Do you remember his name?'

'No… he did mention it but I can't remember,' replied Porter.

'Was it Bevan?'

'Yeah… that was it.'

'This man that you met with the night before your girlfriend's murder is a known criminal. He's been linked with multiple crimes but never convicted.'

'What crimes?'

Wilkins frowned before replying.

'He's a suspect in several open cases, so I shouldn't discuss it really. I will say that he's not the kind of man you can trust.'

'Like I said… I barely know the guy.'

'You just had one drink together?'

'Yeah.'

'I counted at least eight…'

'Well… maybe…'

'Very well. I'll be in touch if there are any developments,' said Wilkins.

The news that Bevan was a known criminal was surprising to Porter. He'd seemed like an unassuming man at the bar, though certainly very opinionated. Had he been responsible in some way to the suspicious circumstances surrounding Cupcake's death? Porter had to find out. He decided that the best way to ask Bevan would be to go back to the bar where they met. Porter spent every night there. Four nights later he reappeared.

Bevan waited by the jukebox once again and scanned the room. He spotted Porter and joined him without hesitation.

'You've caused me a lot of trouble Porter… if that is your real name.'

'Of course it's my real name. Why wouldn't I tell you my name?'

'You owe me fifty thousand dollars. I don't work pro bono. It's kind of a rule of mine. No exceptions.'

'For what?' asked Porter.

'For the hit I did for you.'

'What? Seriously? You killed her? I didn't ask you to kill anyone,' he replied quietly.

'You didn't have to! I was hired for a job and told to meet my employer at the bar. You waved me over.'

'I didn't wave you over…' insisted Porter.

'You indicated me over. You asked for a whisky… which is code for a hit… and then you told me about your girl problem.'

'This is insane.'

'You asked me to kill her! The job was paid for so I took her out. Imagine my surprise when the real client got in touch.'

'I don't know anything about this…'

'I had to return their money…'

'No… no… no…' Porter was in shock.

'Yes… so I had to meet them, apologise and then do their job last night.'

'I thought you said you were a musician…'

'I told you I don't do that anymore.'

Porter couldn't believe it.

'I don't have that kind of money,' he replied, still flabbergasted by the price.

'You've seen my face, friend. You know too much. If you don't find that kind of money… I'll have to make an exception to my pro bono rule.'

'You'd kill me over a misunderstanding?' asked Porter.

'I've killed for less.'

'You murdered my girlfriend and now you want me to pay you for it? I didn't want her dead.'

'Yes you did.'

'No…'

'Then you shouldn't have asked for a whisky. I'll give you a week. Find the money or the next time you see me I'll reunite you and Cupcake for good.'

Porter packed a bag and fled. Without Cupcake there was nothing left for him here. Once his disappearance was discovered Wilkins called his phone consistently, but he never answered. Porter had discarded it in a dumpster to avoid being tracked. Bevan suspected he would run. Like a detective following a cheating husband he hid in the shadows, watching and waiting for his chance to pounce.

Porter's body was found two days later when he failed to check out of his discount motel room. His face had been caved in and his wallet had been taken. Wilkins was notified and due to insufficient evidence the case was unsolved.

PARTY FAVOURS

It was two days before little Brady's fourth birthday and his mother Jane was stressing out. The cake wasn't holding together and she was propping up one side of it with toothpicks out of desperation. Eventually it was structurally sound enough to go into the fridge. She wondered if it looked enough like a truck, which had been the brief from Brady. How had her mother made her a special homemade cake every year when she was a child? Jane had a full album of birthday cakes alone, each more impressive than the last.

Every year she would volunteer to help but Jane felt enlisting the aid of her mother was akin to cheating. Even though none of the other mothers at the party would know it, the victory would have been a hollow one.

She poked her head into her son's bedroom. Brady's slightly snotty nose was restricting his airway, but not enough for her to worry. If she tried to wipe his nose she'd risk waking him and she needed him well rested. Brady was going through an attention-seeking phase. While he wasn't unbearable, he was certainly making her question whether she wanted another baby.

A nearby flush startled Jane as her husband Chris stepped out of the toilet. In his hand was an IPad.

'How long have you been in there?' she asked.

'Not long.'

'I made the cake… I thought you were putting Brady to bed,' added Jane, trying to put a timeline on her husband's activities.

'Yeah he went to sleep and I snuck away.'

Jane stepped past him and into the bathroom. Chris washed his hands and the two started brushing their teeth.

'I've got to start that book your mother lent me,' said Jane after she spat toothpaste into the sink.

'Just tell her you finished it and it was really good,' offered Chris.

'I can't do that… she'll want to discuss it.'

They both paused when they heard Brady stirring in his bed. He moaned twice, perhaps due to a bad dream, and then went back to sleep. The outburst was enough to make Chris and Jane reduce the volume of their conversation.

'How did the cake turn out?' asked Chris.

'Fine. It's in the fridge if you want to look,' said Jane.

'Nah, I'll just look later. It will be a nice surprise.'

Chris had a childlike way of looking at the world. At Brady's third birthday party he'd dressed as a clown and played games with the kids for hours, including *Froggy Froggy can I cross the river?* and *What's the time Mr Wolf?* He was definitely the fun parent, which often made Jane feel like the bossy one.

In the bed she picked up the borrowed novel and opened it a measly twelve pages in. Chris snuggled up to her.

'I thought we were going to spend tonight together.'

'I'm just feeling so tired Chris. And Sunday is such a big day,' said Jane, realising her eyes couldn't focus on the page in front of her.

'It's Friday night. I though we could blow off some steam.'

'Maybe next week, okay? After the party.'

'I'll believe that when I see it,' replied Chris.

'What's wrong with you?' she asked her husband. His evening seemed significantly less stressful to Jane, what with an exhausted Brady falling straight to sleep and Chris retiring to the toilet for goodness knows how long.

'Nothing. It's fine,' he shot back.

'Look… I would… it's just that I feel like there are still a million things to do in the morning. We've got to set up the decorations… you've got them in your car right?'

'No… I'll go pick some up tomorrow.'

'The party is at eleven on Sunday Chris!'

'It's fine! I'll be up early,' he said. 'It will all get done.'

'I'm just feeling a little overwhelmed,' said Jane.

'Well why don't we have sex? Maybe I can *underwhelm* you again…'

She laughed and kissed her husband goodnight.

'Not tonight hon.'

Chris and his wife lived in an apartment building in the city. It made light work of his commute. This meant extra time for himself here and there. Chris liked to jog with Mr. Oak from apartment 3B. He played tennis with Evan Cripps from 5A about once a month and dropped in on old Francis Durwood in 2E as often as he could. Anything to avoid being at home. Chris hadn't taken to parenthood naturally. Jane had accepted that Brady was an adjustment for Chris. He'd taken a lot of convincing to agree to have a baby in the first place. His lifestyle had always been minimalist, and a wife and child had added countless clutter to his home. He didn't own a lot of things, preferring to fill his walls with experiences. These days Chris liked to pretend he was a bachelor again. It was easier than admitting his might have made a mistake.

Mr. Oak was nowhere to be seen and so he went on a run by himself. He passed the dog park and caught the eye of several women as he went. Chris liked to feel attractive to the opposite sex, which was a driving force behind his healthy routine.

When he returned he spotted Mr. Oak and his younger wife on their way out.

'Got a run in then?' asked Mr. Oak.

'Yeah… when I can. Where are you two off to today?'

'Shopping it seems.'

Chris said goodbye and wandered to the elevator. Mr. Oak was more under the thumb than most. He was glad his own marital binds still felt loose.

The elevator doors were being held open for him as he approached. The woman doing the holding was absolutely stunning.

'Thanks,' said Chris as he stepped inside.

'No problem. What floor?' she returned.

'The fifth.'

She pressed the button on his behalf.

'Are you new to the building?' he asked.

'My husband and I have leased an apartment on the sixth floor. I see you're married also?'

'Yes. A couple of years now.'

'And do you like it? Being here in the building I mean… not your marriage.' She smiled.

'Yeah.'

The elevator stopped at the fifth floor and the doors opened for Chris.

'Well nice to meet you,' he said as he took a single step towards the opening. He was only able to make it that far because he was intercepted. Without warning the woman kissed him on the mouth. Chris was startled but kissed her back. The intensity between them grew and the elevator doors closed once more, sealing them inside.

'What's your name?' she asked.

'Chris.'

'Chris what?'

'Chris Walters.'

'I'm Lila. *Now* we've met.'

The doors opened once again, this time on the sixth floor, where Lila strode away confidently. Chris was left stunned as he travelled back down to Jane and Brady on the fifth floor. He got straight in the shower and thought about Lila. If Jane noticed the increased duration of the wash she didn't mention it.

'Your phone pinged,' his wife said after he returned to the kitchen.

'Thanks. How's Brady doing?'

'He's alright. I parked him in front of the TV so I could make lolly bags for the kids.'

'How many kids from daycare are we expecting tomorrow anyway?' asked Chris.

'All of them.'

'*All* of them? How many is that?'

'Twenty or so. It doesn't matter how many actually turn up. It's just going to be at the park.'

Chris checked his phone and saw a Facebook friend request from Lila Alice. He was suddenly filled with a nervous excitement. The profile picture matched the woman from the elevator. Chris walked over to the sofa and sat down next to his son. His new position allowed him to look at the screen without his wife catching on. Lila's profile was sparse. There was no sign of her husband in any of the pictures. He accepted the request and the messages started almost immediately.

Hi Chris.

Hi Lila.

It was really nice meeting you.

I think I'm going to like living here in the building.

I like it here too.

You should know that I don't do that with all the neighbours.

I'm not sure what came over me.

It's alright. It was a pretty memorable moment.

Can I say something? I'm just going to say it. You have a really great natural smell.

I'd just been running!

I really liked it. You're in great shape too.

Thanks. I try. Do you like to jog?

Not really. I like to stay in shape though.

That's good. Do you work in the city?

No but my husband does.

What does he do?

Ignores me.

Sorry to hear that.

What's your wife like?

She's pretty good. A bit stressed at the moment.

I'd be stressed too if my husband looked as good as you.

Ha ha. Very funny. It's just a busy weekend for us.

Are you stressed out too?

Nah. I'm okay. Thanks for asking.

Well if you start to get stressed... you should message me.

'Was it important?' asked Jane as she approached the sofa.

'Huh?'

'The message?'

'It was nothing.'

'So are you going to help me out today or what?' asked Jane.

'With what?'

'Your son's birthday!'

'That's tomorrow though.'

'But we're getting things ready *today*.'

Jane supplied him with a list of things to buy including snacks, balloons and a piñata. Chris gave his son a kiss on the head and took the opportunity to sneak away again. He decided to message Lila from the elevator.

I'm in the elevator again.

Going down.

That's our spot x

You're such a flirt.

☺

I can't help myself.

☺

Chris picked up healthy fruit snacks, chips and soft drink. He also grabbed a bottle of alcohol for himself. He loved to have a drink in the evening, even though Jane would never join him. He wondered whether Lila liked to drink. He was enjoying their ongoing flirtation.

In the evening he kept checking his phone. He was pleased to see Lila was online. Chris wondered whether she was scrolling through his pictures, and whether he was on her mind at all. It had been years since anyone other than Jane had kissed him. It was an exciting sensation, certainly more exciting than a four year olds birthday party could ever be. Even if it was his own son's.

Jane seemed fed up but Chris was oblivious. He was staring at his phone, completely zoned out.

'How did you go today?' she asked.

'Yeah, fine.'

'Did you get everything?'

'Almost. I'll get the piñata tomorrow. They were closed.'

'What were you doing all day?' asked Jane.

'Why are you snapping at me?'

'You've been out *all day*... I just figured you would have-'

'Well I didn't,' interrupted Chris.

'Are you going to spend *any* time with us this weekend? Or any weekend?'

'Ugh... why are you getting mad at me?'

'It's your son's birthday. I just thought you'd want to be a part of it.'

Chris finished his drink and retreated to the toilet. He pulled out his phone and messaged Lila.

Alright I'm stressed. You told me to message.

Do you want to meet up?

Where? Is your husband home?

Yes. Is your wife?

Yes.

Meet me in the elevator.

Ok. Five minutes.

Brady was fast asleep with his hands resting at his sides. This boy was fussy for a year or so but now he was so well behaved that he almost put himself to bed at night. Chris didn't see an issue. He'd given Jane a pleasant baby, a beautiful apartment and years of faithfulness. Enough was enough. He needed a break from their routine. Chris needed a break from his wife.

He called the elevator and was pleased to see Lila's face when the doors splayed apart. She was dressed in a dark silk shirt and fashionable pants that flared out at the ankles. She smiled and he moved towards her. They started kissing passionately, and Chris pressed Lila against the wall. As the elevator started to move she reached down and pressed the emergency stop button.

'I don't want anyone to interrupt us,' she said quickly.

Chris stuck his fingers down and into the front of her pants as they continued to kiss. Lila moaned at his touch and grabbed at his crotch. She could feel him growing against her. Lila opened her shirt and unclipped her bra at the front. Chris cupped her breasts in his hands as she undid his belt. Soon they were both almost naked, except for his socks and her shirt, which he'd opened. She lifted her leg as he pressed her against the mirrored wall of the elevator. He slid inside and they stared at each other for a moment. Lila's mouth stayed open for each accompanying thrust. She smelled intoxicating, like some kind of artificial flora. She wrapped her legs around him, her heel landing between the cheeks of his buttocks. They climaxed within seconds of one another.

It wasn't awkward afterwards like it had been with previous new lovers. Chris dressed himself and smiled at Lila.

'What are you smiling at?' she asked.

'You. I can't believe I just met you this morning.'

'It felt so natural though, didn't it?'

'It did, yeah.'

'Listen… I want to see you again Chris. Would that be okay?'

'Definitely.'

'I have to go back to my apartment now. I'll message you, alright?'

'Okay,' replied Chris.

Lila kissed him deeply before saying goodnight. It made him realise that at some point he and Jane stopped kissing with tongue. It felt so foreign to French kiss Lila now, but he was happy to do it.

Back at home Jane had given up and gone to bed. He couldn't tell if she was asleep as he tucked in beside her and dozed off easily.

On the morning of Brady's birthday party Chris woke up alone. He could hear his wife in the bathroom bathing their now four year old. Brady loved baths and was co-operating happily.

He looked over to his phone and saw an urgent message from Lila.

9-1-1!

What is it? Did your husband find out?

Worse. Can you meet me?

It's not a good time.

It's important! Please!

He reluctantly agreed to meet with Lila. Chris threw on a sweatshirt, grabbed his wallet, phone and keys and snuck away. He could hear his son splashing in the bath as he closed the front door. Brady's party was at eleven and he could say he went out for the piñata. Jane might be upset that he didn't pop his head in to say hello, but he could pretend that he was still hung up on the fight from the day before. He met Lila in the foyer. She looked worried.

'What's going on?' he asked.

'We're fucked.'

'What? What are you on about?'

'The building super was notified when I pushed the button and stopped the elevator last night. He investigated and saw us on the surveillance camera.'

'Oh fuck.'

'Yeah… and now he's blackmailing me for the tape.'

'He can't do that.'

'He's threatening to leak it. Chris, my husband can't find out about it. He just can't.'

'Fuck… how much is he asking for?'

'Ten grand. I can't move that much money without my husband noticing. I might be able to get half of that.'

'That's steep.'

'I need the other half from you. I can pay you back.'

'What? Why?'

'Because I need it.'

'I shouldn't have to…' he trailed off.

'If I got pregnant would you offer to pay for half of the abortion?' asked Lila.

'I guess so.' He hated the idea of more children depending on him.

'Well this is the same thing. We pay half each to make this go away.'

'I guess.'

'If this gets out and you ruin my marriage I'll make sure your wife sees the footage too. Don't make me do that Chris. Don't spoil this affair before it's even really begun.'

Chris knew that he didn't want his wife to see images of him, almost completely nude, having sex in an elevator with a perfect stranger. The footage would be time-stamped too, and Jane would know that he was unfaithful on the eve of their son's birthday. It was not a good situation to be in, so he reluctantly agreed to pay half of the money. He hoped that the five thousand dollars would be an investment in this affair. He wanted to sleep with Lila again. Chris was thankful that he still had his own savings account. Which meant his wife wouldn't be able to check up on him.

'Okay… so are you meeting him or what?' asked Chris.

'No. It's Sunday. I have to direct deposit the money via my bank app. So if you send it to me, I can send the ten grand all together.'

Chris sent her the money.

'Don't worry,' Lila said. 'I'll be in touch again when my husband's out of town… if you want to get together again?'

'That would be good.'

Lila wandered away.

'Where have you been?' asked Jane when he returned to their apartment on the fifth floor.

'I just got this,' he replied, holding up a piñata, which he'd hastily bought after seeing Lila.

'And you didn't think to say good morning to us? To tell me you were going out?'

'I was quick, wasn't I? You barely noticed I was gone,' replied Chris, who was happy he had gotten away with this latest deception.

'Brady's in the living room.'

'Okay…'

'So go in and say happy birthday to him!' commanded Jane, shaking her head at her husband.

Brady was indifferent to his presence. He was glued to Sunday morning cartoons. They didn't have a strong bond, and neither party minded. Jane loaded his arms with supplies and they all headed out to the park for Brady's fourth birthday.

As they set up the balloons and Chris hung the piñata it occurred to him that he'd never looked at the cake, which Jane had slaved over two nights before. Upon inspection he liked it a lot, but couldn't tell her that without revealing the degree to which he'd been distracted.

Guests arrived and Chris found himself feeling uncomfortable. Jane kept suggesting that he take the lead with some party games. He didn't want to play games like he had the previous year. Chris had been on ecstasy at the time and running around with children seemed like fun. It had been a passing phase for him. Chris had given up when Reece Menzies, a local dealer who'd been staying in 7C, moved away. Without the influence of the drug he found the idea of games ridiculous, the noise unnecessary and interacting with other parents unbearable.

Chris suggested the kids take turns at the piñata, which they quickly lined for. Each hopeful swing did minimal damage. It took nearly twenty minutes before the cracks appeared and the piñata was ready to burst. Jane gave the bat to Brady so that the birthday boy could deliver the killer blow. On his third swing it burst open and showered the guests with treats. However instead of the traditional lolly-related contents, this piñata was full of condoms and custom made penis-shaped gummies.

The sight of twenty infants putting edible genitals in their mouths was too much for most of the conservative parents to handle. They scooped up their children one by one and started to leave, some hurling abuse at Chris as they went.

'Where did you get that piñata Chris?' demanded Jane. 'Did you get it from the place I asked you to?'

He hadn't.

His mind had been on the impending blackmail and he'd purchased the first piñata he'd seen.

'It might have been from a novelty shop,' he confessed.

'What? Are you serious?'

'I didn't really think it would matter,' said Chris.

'Well it did!' shouted Jane as she stormed off, collecting condoms from the grass as she moved. She forced her fingers into one child's mouth and removed a banana-scented prophylactic from him. The boy had chewed it so much that it was now useless as birth control.

Chris liked to make memories, favouring experiences over material things, but this was one weekend he wanted to forget.

That night he messaged Lila but there was no response. Her Facebook account had been deactivated. Chris started to loiter in the lobby and ride the elevator in the hope that Lila would appear. It was two weeks later when he saw the building super and decided to confront him about the surveillance footage.

'Hello,' he said.

'Hello Mr. Walters how are you?' the super replied.

'Fine… thanks… I wanted to talk to you about Lila…' it occurred to him that he didn't know her last name. He presumed that Lila Alice was her first and middle name, from the Facebook profile she'd used. 'Lila from the sixth floor.'

'Um… I'm not sure I've met her yet.'

'She moved in with her husband recently?'

'I don't think anybody has moved in or out of the sixth floor in years,' the man replied with a shake of his head.

'She had a conversation with you about the… elevator?'

'Nope. Maybe she spoke to someone else?'

'No… I guess I was mistaken. Thanks anyway.'

Lila Alice was a con artist that had posed as a resident of their apartment building. She'd targeted Chris specifically and invented the lie about the surveillance tape in order to take five thousand dollars from him. Lila wasn't even close to her real name.

While she'd quickly forgotten about him and the grift she'd successfully executed, Chris never stopped looking for Lila. His marriage to Jane lasted until the week of Brady's seventh birthday, when he was asked to move out of the apartment.

INSPIRATION

'The book is a hit Teri, number one in all the demographics we wanted!'

'That's brilliant news Morty. I shall have to tell Alan at once.'

Teri Banks phoned her husband at three thirty in the afternoon. After a few rings she started to wonder what he could be doing. Perhaps he was in the bath. *Why was he always in the bath though?* wondered Teri. Alan had experienced a psychotic episode and now believed the bathtub to be the safest place in their home. Their two children had grown up and moved out years ago. Teri and Alan were now well and truly alone. The empty rooms had made Alan mad at first, attempting a flurry of hobbies and activities to fill the space left by parenting. Neither of their sons was particularly dependent and they called very infrequently to check in. Alan's realisation that his death would one day arrive had caused him to break mentally. This snap had occurred on his fifty-third birthday and he'd been rubbish to live with ever since. Teri had retired from her office job to take care of him, which he'd hated. Alan spent so much time moping around that Teri wound up taking on a hobby of her own – writing. She seemed to have a knack for it and secured a publisher based on just a few short sample chapters. Alan was bitter with her instant success and drank a bottle of wine every night. Sometimes in a drunken stupor he threatened to kill himself but soon Teri learned that it was mostly a cry for attention.

As usual Alan did not answer the phone.

'I'll just tell him later,' said Teri as she set the receiver back down.

'They want you to appear on some daytime television shows as well as a plethora of book signings. Do you think you'll be able to leave Alan for a month or so?' asked Morty.

I'd love to leave Alan she thought to herself. Teri had often thought about having an affair with her agent Morty Herman. He had greying hair and some wrinkles around his mouth from over-smiling, but he was so charming that she often wondered what it would be like to kiss him. Perhaps a month alone together on the road would finally spark something between them.

'He'll have to be. I can't miss this opportunity.'

When she returned home that evening Teri found Alan alone on the sofa. She took pause and wondered how much longer she could put up with his antics. Maybe a month away was exactly what he needed to get out of this depressing funk.

'Hello dear,' she said as she put down her bag. 'How was your day?'

'Meaningless,' her husband replied.

'Perhaps if you went outside for a while you'd discover some meaning.'

'I don't feel up to it,' said Alan, sounding like Eeyore from *Winnie the Pooh*.

She placed her new book down in front of him, ensuring the glossy cover was aimed towards his slumped face. Alan looked at it but did not change position. The cover featured a man in a white business shirt, face obscured by shadow, holding a cleaver in one hand. It reminded Alan of every made for TV movie about a husband who turns out to be a liar and eventually a murderer.

'It's all finished then?' he asked.

'It's been finished for ages Alan… It's been on the shelves for weeks as a hardcover. You really don't listen when I speak, do you? This is the mock up for international markets.'

The cover was fairly similar to the previous one but Alan wouldn't have known that. He hadn't paid attention to the launch, or the upswing of sales, or the media attention. Alan just wanted it all to go away. Teri was just trying to engage him. She didn't know what she wanted him to say exactly. She wanted some validation, perhaps a small congratulatory moment for her dedication and hard work. Alan returned a hum, and then a small grunt. It was nothing. She floated to the kitchen where she found a sink of dishes that Alan had left throughout the day. Their marriage was past any need for courtesy. Alan no longer wanted anything from Teri, which left them at a stalemate.

She found a pile of mail that had been sent over by Morty. It was from her fans. Some were printed and some were old-fashioned snail mail that had been sent to the publisher. Teri browsed a few of the printed emails before setting them aside. She decided the letters might be more fruitful, perhaps even scratching her itchy ego that Alan had ignored.

The first few letters were glowing with praise. They spoke about the female lead in the novel and how fantastic she was. Some comments were about the twist ending while others focussed on the evil male villain and his weapon of choice: the cleaver. The next letter made her gasp. Inside a hand-written letter was a photograph of a man's genitals. She felt herself blush. The attached letter stressed how beautiful Teri was on the back cover and offered to meet her anytime she wanted. She was flattered. It was fine to fantasize about Morty or even this faceless stranger privately, but the reality was that she was still married to Alan. She slipped the photograph and letter into her desk drawer for safekeeping.

The next letter had no return address on the back. She opened it cautiously, knowing that the publisher had not vetted her mail in any way. Looking inside she saw no white powder or immediate threat, and so she removed the correspondence. It was written in the style of a ransom note, with each letter cut out from a magazine or newspaper. It read:

HeLLo Teri BANkS.

WhEN DiD YOU KnoW

I WAS A Killer?

S

Teri hesitated and put the letter down on her desk. She wondered how she should proceed. Based on his previous lethargic response she knew that Alan would be predictably useless. *Should she inform the police?* While the letter felt sinister it wasn't actually a threat, more of a curiosity. She decided to call Morty and explain the situation to him.

'So it says *when did you know*... like you *know* this individual?' asked Morty.

'Yes... and they've signed it with an *S*.'

'So check your Rolodex, who do you know with an *S*?'

A quick check revealed many options, both with S surnames or first names.

'Are you suggesting that one of these people is a killer?' she asked.

'I'm not suggesting it, they are. They are asking when *you* knew.'

'But I don't know.'

'But they think you do,' added Morty.

'The letter was sent to the publisher. They must have read my novel,' said Teri.

'Yes, that's plausible. There are a lot of whack jobs out there. If they sent it to us maybe you don't know them at all.'

'So they've identified with the killer in the book, which means they are male,' said Teri.

'Not necessarily… I'm sure there are lots of women that identify as men… you know… it's all different these days… I don't know what's politically correct anymore,' he confessed.

'But it's *probably* a man.'

'I'd say so,' replied Morty.

'So they… *he* perhaps… has read my book and thinks I'm writing about him? Like I'm documenting his murders,' she said, slightly shaking at the notion. 'It's a work of fiction!'

'Like I said… there are a lot of whack jobs out there.'

Morty promised to contact the police and make a formal complaint. He encouraged her to photograph the letter and then place it in a zip lock bag so it could be checked for fingerprints. Teri complied. When she got off the phone with Morty she opened the door to the study and found Alan listening against it. He nearly toppled over when she opened it, giving them both a fright.

'What are you doing?' she asked.

'Nothing,' he replied and slunk away. It was the most he'd moved in days.

Her publishing team were hoping that Teri would consider writing a sequel to her novel. At the conclusion of her first book the villain was behind bars and the female housewife had started studying to become a police officer, lending itself to the idea of serialisation.

'In your second book you could have your lead, who is now on the force, find a copycat killer… or a new killer, it doesn't matter… but it leads her to talk to the bad guy from the first book. He's still in prison. It's like *Silence of the Lambs*. It takes a killer to catch a killer.' Morty was beaming with enthusiasm for his unoriginal idea.

'It's… an interesting thought Morty. It's not really the way I work. I need more time to figure out a second book. I don't know if I'll want to write another thriller like that.'

'You're good at this Teri. You should consider that when you sit down to write. This is what is selling for us now, and while I don't want to pigeonhole you or stifle you creatively, this is the kind of book that we're willing to pay you an advance on,' stated Morty. At the end of the day it was still a business to him. This wasn't the version of Morty that Teri fantasised about. She liked it when he praised her. He made her feel like a goddess in a way that Alan hadn't in years.

'I'll think about it.'

The issue was that whenever Teri sat down at her computer to write she felt empty. She thought about reading another book, perhaps something to inspire a story, but she couldn't. The truth was that she didn't want to copy another writer's ideas – even subconsciously. She needed to sit down and think about her *own* experiences. She had found her first novel that way after all.

The phone rang in the living room and Alan made no attempt to get it. It was never for him and he knew it. On the rare occasion that one of their sons called they wanted to talk to their mother anyway. Teri was grateful for the interruption. It was better than staring at the blank screen.

'Hello?'

'Hello Teri.'

The voice on the other end of the call was being modified by a device, resulting in a deep robotic tone that was surprisingly sinister.

'Who is this? she demanded.

'Did you get my letter?' came the reply.

'Do I know you? S? Is that your name?' asked Teri, desperately seeking answers.

'You know me well enough to write a story about me.'

'But I didn't write my novel about you…'

'You can lie to yourself all you want. I know the truth.'

'What do you want?'

'You'll know soon enough.'

The call was terminated abruptly, leaving Teri perplexed.

The next day she found herself in Morty's office.

'You look awful,' he said.

'I feel it. I couldn't sleep at all.'

Teri couldn't help but feel violated. This stalker knew where she lived. He'd called her at home. It was different when he was sending a letter to the publishers. Teri didn't feel safe and Alan was as useless as ever.

'So what do you want to do? Go back to the police again?'

'I guess that's best.'

The police determined that the individual harassing her was an imminent threat and, because the Mayor was a fan of her novel, they positioned an officer in an unmarked car outside her house. In the event of another phone call Teri was to signal the plain-clothes officer with a walkie-talkie so they could listen in and track the call. After a week of tension, and no phone calls, the officer was removed.

She'd informed her husband about the stalker but he'd made no attempts to console her. Morty, in contrast had been on the phone to Teri almost every night. While she wanted to cancel the upcoming book tour Morty increased security and insisted it was the right thing to do. Alan, clearly miffed about being left alone, increased his bathing schedule.

The first stop of the tour was to be her hometown. Teri Banks had amassed a ton of fans at home due to the fact that her late mother had been a well-loved politician and the press still loved to write about her whenever they could.

It was at Teri's second book signing, which took place at a bookshop near her childhood home, that she received a blast from the past. In the line, waiting to have his book signed was her high school boyfriend Jerry. He looked as handsome as ever, and greeted her with a wave.

'Hi there! Fancy seeing you here,' said Jerry with a grin.

Teri was immediately attracted to him, and stood up to hug him.

'Jerry! How long has it been?'

'Too long. Congratulations on the book. I'll admit I haven't read it yet but it looks great!'

'Thanks Jerry. It's so good to see you.'

She wondered why they had broken up and was pleased to find his left hand was wedding ring free.

'Would you like to catch up later?' she asked, forgetting all about Alan and Morty.

'I'd love to.'

She told Jerry to give his details to Morty and that she would see him after the signing.

Overall it was a solid showing. Three hundred or so locals came out at lunchtime to get their novels signed and see if the now famous Teri Banks remembered them. When she approached Morty to get her ex-boyfriend's details he hesitated.

'Teri, with this stalker situation I'm not comfortable sending you out on your own.'

'I'll be fine Morty. If you're that concerned why don't you have one of the security guards follow at a distance?'

Teri met up with Jerry at a café. He'd changed into a smart blazer.

'Who are you trying to impress?' she asked as she gave him another hug.

'You, of course!'

The two sat down opposite each other. Teri could feel her face strain against her huge smile. It occurred to her that she hadn't smiled like that in a long time. Her marriage to Alan had become a failure and it was probably time to pull the plug. She was still vivacious enough to receive unsolicited nudes in the mail after all!

'Do you remember this place?' he asked.

'Of course. It's barely changed.'

The room was purple and splashed on every available surface was a different black and white photograph. She counted twelve larger pieces and seven or eight smaller ones. It had been a popular hangout for artistic kids when Teri was growing up and looking around at the clientele not much had changed.

'We used to come here a lot. I try not to but I think about you sometimes when I'm here,' admitted Jerry.

'You do?'

'It's hard not to. You're still on the wall,' he said, indicating to a black and white photograph of a woman's bust. It was artistically shot, with gloved hands covering the nipples.

'Oh my God. I'd forgotten about that picture.'

'I haven't!' he said with a laugh.

'That's because you took it! Oh I can't believe it's still up. This is mortifying.'

'Relax… nobody knows it's you.'

'You know it's me! And that's one too many I think,' she said as she felt her face blush.

'I won't tell.'

'Good.'

They ordered coffee and talked about high school, reminiscing about the classmates that they'd each kept in touch with. At one point his leg came to rest against hers and neither of them moved away.

'And how are you... I mean... how is your marriage?' he asked, a little too hopefully.

'It's not much of a marriage anymore,' confessed Teri.

'I'm sorry to hear that.'

'No you're not.'

'No... I'm not,' replied Jerry.

'Did you ever get married?'

'I was married for almost a year... but she passed away. Brain cancer.'

'Oh that's horrible.'

'It was the worst.'

'Listen... I know this is happening quickly... but would you want to see me again?' asked Teri.

'Yes.'

She phoned her husband that night, hoping to declare her desire for a divorce, but Alan didn't answer the phone.

Morty was extremely inquisitive after her date with Jerry. It was almost as if he knew he'd been the natural and obvious successor to Teri's heart and was now threatened by a newcomer. She was thrilled with his jealous streak.

'Don't worry about it, okay?'

'We're leaving in the morning Teri. Do… whatever it is you need to do tonight.'

She raised an eyebrow.

'That sounds so sinister Morty. I'm a married woman.'

Her agent could see right through her. Teri wasn't very good at hiding it, and frankly she felt like she deserved some happiness after almost thirty years with Alan. Now, with this sudden influx of attention she considered kissing Morty, but decided against it. He still worked for her after all.

That night there was a knock on her hotel room door.

'Alan?' Teri couldn't believe her husband had left the house, let alone found her so resourcefully.

'Hello dear. May I come in?'

Teri stepped back and closed the door behind him. She checked her phone, happily finding a message from Jerry stating that he was running late. She messaged him back and told him that she would drive to his place, citing that she had to do a phone interview before she could leave. While Alan sat down on the couch at the foot of her bed she received a thumbs up emoji from Jerry.

She'd avoided a very difficult encounter between her soon to be ex-husband and her ex-boyfriend, and if she had anything to do with it, soon to be new lover.

'How did you know I was here?' asked Teri.

'I called Morty after I found this,' he said thrusting a piece of paper at her.

It was the letter and accompanying nude image from her desk.

'You went through my desk?' she asked.

'It was the only way to find out the truth,' he replied.

'And what is the truth?'

'You're cheating on me, aren't you? Admit it!'

'I'm not cheating on you Alan. This was fan mail.'

'You can't expect me to believe that…'

'Honestly, someone sent it to me,' said Teri.

'You get fan mail?'

'Yes.'

'From actual fans? Of your writing?' demanded Alan, who seemed confused with the process.

'Yes! People like my novel. Have you even read it?'

'No.'

'And you're meant to be my husband… arguably my biggest fan.'

'You haven't wanted me to be your husband for a long time,' he stated.

'That wasn't true… but now it is. You pushed me away, didn't you? Well… be careful what you wish for Alan Banks.'

'So I was right?'

'Yes… I suppose you're right. I don't want to stay married to you anymore. Does that make you happy? But I haven't cheated on you once during our entire relationship.'

'I don't believe you.'

'I don't care what you believe. I don't want to see you again Alan. When the book tour is over I want to come home to an empty house.'

'If you divorce me I'll get half the profits from your book! You don't want that, do you Teri?'

'It's a small price to pay.'

Alan looked defeated. He stopped arguing and removed the car keys from his pocket.

'You drove here?' she asked, recognising the key chain.

'Yeah. Have fun with your adoring public.'

And with that he was gone. Teri waited about ten minutes before she called a taxi and went to see Jerry. The two made passionate love that night as if no time had passed. Teri felt young and free.

The next morning Morty called her.

'Where are you? When you didn't answer I had to get the hotel staff to let me into your suite.'

'I'm fine… I'm with Jerry.'

'This is not acceptable behaviour. I was worried about you,' replied Morty.

'I'll come back soon, okay?'

She left a note for Jerry, thanking him for the pleasant evening, and snuck out while he slept. When she returned to the hotel Morty looked depressed.

'It's okay Morty, I'm here. Nothing happened to me.'

'Teri… its Alan. He's dead.'

She didn't know where to look.

'Are you joking?' she asked.

'I'm so sorry,' said Morty.

'How?'

'He crashed into a tree.'

'Last night?'

'Yes.'

As the details were revealed Teri found herself crying. In a way it was exactly what she'd wished for during her seemingly endless marriage. She felt awful because she was free at the ultimate cost to Alan. Her stomach was in knots about their final conversation and the hurt that he would have endured. She cried as she wondered whether he'd driven into a tree deliberately, or whether it was an accident. Either way it wouldn't change the fact that Alan was dead.

'The police are going to be in touch with more details as the investigation continues. Is there anything I can do?'

'Yeah… cancel the book tour.'

Teri went back to her house but couldn't stay there. Alan was everywhere and it was overwhelming. She called Jerry who answered straight away.

'How are you?' he asked.

'Awful. I don't know what to do.'

'Can I come and see you?' he asked.

'Yes.'

Jerry arrived on a wintery morning and brought a gift. Teri opened it once they were safely inside. It was the sexy black and white picture that Teri had taken in her youth.

'From the café?' she asked.

'Yeah… I had to buy it back from them,' said Jerry with a smile.

'Thanks.'

'I just wanted to remind you of that girl you used to be. She's still in there you know.'

'I know.'

'It's kind of like the woman in your book. She loses her husband and then she realises her potential by the end.'

Teri's phone rang. It was Morty. She excused herself and walked into the kitchen.

'Hi Morty.'

'Listen to me carefully. Someone cut the brakes on Alan's car. The police have a suspicious character on a security camera the night he died. I haven't seen the footage but it sounds like your ex-boyfriend Jerry.'

Jerry smiled at Teri from across the room.

Could it be true?

'Morty… I don't think I can talk about my second novel right now. I'm just not in a good headspace.'

'He's there now isn't he? It's going to be alright… just keep him talking, okay?' pleaded a stressed Morty.

'Okay… maybe tomorrow we can discuss it,' she replied.

'I'm calling the police. They'll be there soon.'

'Thanks Morty... you too.'

Teri hung up the phone and tried to remain nonchalant.

'Did you say you've been reading my book?' she asked Jerry.

'Oh yes... I've started it. Did I tell you that?'

'But you just... mentioned the ending...'

Jerry's grin widened.

'I did, didn't I?'

'Is there something you'd like to say to me... Mr S was it?' asked Teri.

'Ah... you got my letter then? I had hoped the publishers would pass it on.'

'This one wasn't like the love letters you used to write me...'

'Well we've both come a long way with our craft. You seem content to write all about me,' said Jerry as he stood up. Teri knew she had to keep him talking until the police arrived.

'Yes... it's interesting that you think it's about you... because it is,' admitted Teri.

'I knew it.'

'Well, I drew inspiration from our high school romance...'

'I recognised so much of *us* in your work,' said Jerry taking another step toward her.

'I'll admit that I've thought about you a lot since our relationship ended. I've fantasised... but the Jerry I wrote about was evil...'

'You've always known me so well. Perhaps on some level you knew what I was capable of.'

'Did you kill your wife? Or did she really die of brain cancer?'

'Ultimately the cancer killed her. But after she died I had nothing left to lose. I've killed a few people… here and there. I'm not ashamed of it. It made me feel something if I'm honest. I never knew anything about them though.'

'You target strangers?'

'Yes… usually. I made an exception for Alan.'

'You cut the brakes?'

'Of course I did. You didn't think he had it in him to kill himself did you?'

There was an odd relief inside Teri.

'Why would you kill my husband?'

'So I could be with you of course. But now that you've figured me out… I guess our story is over as well.'

'You don't have to do this Jerry… I won't turn you in.'

'No? I'll bet if I let you live you'll write another novel about me. I can't be having that.'

Jerry took deliberate strides towards Teri just as the police burst through the door of her home. Two armed officers pointed weapons at Jerry and he fell to his knees. He shook his head in disbelief, surprised that she'd outmanoeuvred him somehow. Before the police took Jerry into custody she needed to ask him one question.

'Why did you call yourself S?' asked Teri.

He hesitated for a moment, considering that his response might incriminate him further. Jerry decided it was too late now, and he may as well be honest.

'Because you used to say I was your soul mate.'

When the police took Jerry away she was suddenly alone in her living room. The black and white portrait stared up at her. She suddenly saw it in a new light, and imagined the piece as the front cover of a novel. Teri wanted to write again. Her writer's block was over.

Following Alan's funeral Teri's publicity tour was back on. The venues were bigger and so were the crowds. Her book was flying off the shelves thanks to the attempt on her life. People had to read the story that drove a man to the point of murder. Morty had secured her a multi-million dollar deal for her second novel, which Teri agreed would be in the same vein as her first. She knew that art would imitate life once again, and that Jerry would be her inspiration.

The book tour was a welcome distraction and before she knew it reporters were peppering Teri with questions.

'Miss Banks! Can you tell us about what you're working on now?'

'Well, as you know I've had some trauma recently. I'm finding my way through it by writing down my experience. I'm hoping to turn my tragedy into art.'

'Does your next novel have a title?'

'Soul mate.' Teri nodded. She was pleased with herself. It was a fine idea that she could build on.

'Hello?'

'Alan? What took you so long to pick up?' asked Teri.

'I was hanging out the washing. What's up?'

'Morty just told me… the book is a hit!'

'Wow! Congratulations my love. So you're number one?' asked Alan.

'Yes… on all the demographics we were hoping for.'

'Amazing. I'm so proud of you Teri.'

'And Alan?'

'Yeah?'

'I might have just had an idea for my next one.'

'That's exciting. Do you kill me off in this one too?' he asked.

'I'm afraid so. Car crash… but don't worry, someone else cut the brakes!'

'That's exciting.'

'Yes… it's rough… the placeholder names are all wrong and it's a bit predictable… but I'll find it.'

'I can't wait to read it,' Alan said gleefully.

Calvin Thompson was a hot guy and he knew it. At the age of seventeen he'd straddled the line between boy and man perfectly, aging himself up with a timeless leather jacket and jeans combination, or downplaying his attractiveness by dressing in his school uniform. There had always been interest from the opposite sex, including two of his high school teachers. He'd lost his virginity at a young age and it had shaped the way he viewed his worth. The unfortunate thing about Calvin was that he was *all* exterior. He spent most of his time trying to become a model, and none of his time on his education. He was the kind of guy that spent an hour shaping his dark hair every morning hoping to be discovered. He found Instagram fame by posing shirtless regularly and grew his fan base to over thirty thousand followers. It wasn't enough for him though. He wanted to be properly famous. The problem with Calvin was that he had no talent. He just expected things to come to him the way women did. When school finished and the modelling world hadn't answered his calls, his father told him he had to contribute to the rent. He was unable to monetise his Instagram account consistently, getting only a few offers for hair gel and laxatives ads, which is how Calvin found himself working at his local supermarket.

That's where he met Norah.

Norah was obsessed with romantic comedies. She'd been conditioned to think that love was the most important currency on Earth. She'd been described in the past by potential suitors as *clingy* and *too much*. Norah believed that her perfect man would appear and that at exactly that moment a hit song would play just for them. She'd worked at the supermarket counter for a few years after school but had been replaced by self-serve machines. This left

Norah packing shelves at night, which suited her now that classes had finished and she could sleep in during the day.

That's when she met Calvin.

The moment they first met was like a fantastic dream for Norah. She was waiting outside the manager's office when Calvin, looking fresh and dreamy like James Dean, stepped through the door. They locked eyes and he smiled a whitened smile at Norah. An Ed Sheeran song played throughout the store speakers as she blushed.

'Oh Calvin, meet Norah,' said the manager. He was good at making polite introductions and terrible at remembering personal information about his employees.

'Hey.' Calvin was so laid back and cool. Norah was intimidated and couldn't reply. She smiled and watched him walk away.

'Wow. He's gorgeous,' she said after he'd left her line of sight.

'Calvin? Yeah he wanted to be an actor or something… didn't work out I guess. Now Norah, we're not going to have any trouble with *this* one are we?'

Her boss was referring to a recent incident involving an employee named Hudson that she had been infatuated with. Norah had 'accidently' followed him into the men's bathroom and stayed an uncomfortably long time. She maintained that it was a misunderstanding but Hudson resigned shortly after the event. She had been given the nickname *Parasite* in the aftermath by some of her peers, because of her aggressive attempts to attach herself to the opposite sex.

'No… no trouble,' she replied.

'Well… and I want you to know I'm on your side here… the company has asked me to provide you with some sexual harassment training.'

'Oh I don't need any, really.'

'I'm afraid that you don't have a say in the matter. The training is mandatory.'

'Really?'

'Now Norah, you'll be paid to partake. It will take place on Friday, instead of your regular shift.'

She rolled her eyes.

'Why can't we just watch a videotape like we did when I got hired?' she asked.

'Well they've changed the policy since… well… *recently*.'

Norah was certainly to blame. The elephant in the room was her behaviour with Hudson.

'I mean… I'd rather work on Friday if I'm being honest.'

'And Calvin will be joining you.'

Norah perked up.

'As a new employee he has to undergo the same training modules as you,' said her boss.

'Oh alright,' she said with a smile, 'if I *must*.'

In the three days before the training Calvin had sex with five different women. Two were scheduled dates, with women he'd been with before, while the remaining conquests came from random encounters. Sometimes Calvin asked one of his dates to take a photo of him for social media. He wished he could make more money from his Instagram account. Calvin wanted to save up enough money to move out of home. His parents couldn't understand his modelling ambition. His father wasn't sure what to do with Calvin. He wasn't competent enough to try University and didn't have the drive to fight his way up a corporate ladder. His interests only seemed to revolve around women or modelling.

Norah's parents were frustrated with her obsession with the opposite sex. She'd discovered boys at the age of twelve when she'd replaced every image on her walls with shirtless men. Although there had only been one formal complaint about her behaviour at work, they had fielded dozens of informal ones. Norah crept into the next-door neighbours bedroom once when he left his window open and was caught. She'd been spotted peering into change rooms, checking men out underwater at the pool and looking at inappropriate material at the public library. Her parents were thankful her crushes were age appropriate and hoped that her explosion of hormones was just a phase she would work through in time.

Both teenagers ultimately wanted attention and validation. Calvin seemingly wanted to continue to prove his worth by bedding as many women as he could until fame came to him. Norah on the other hand wanted to be seen, and wished for affection in an effort to find her one true love.

That Friday the training was taking place off site at a function room, hired specifically by head office. Norah had incorrectly assumed that she would be alone with Calvin when in fact the supermarket had asked a dozen employees to participate. She didn't recognise anyone else and soon learned that they were from other locations around town. Norah felt overdressed for the event, noting that most participants had elected to wear jeans. Calvin removed his jacket to reveal a short-sleeved shirt that he'd rolled up the sleeves up on, exposing most of his shoulders.

Norah lingered nearby and when he took a seat she filled the one beside him.

'Oh hey. Nicole was it?' asked Calvin.

'Norah.'

'Right.'

'Are you super psyched for this training?' she asked.

'Beats packing shelves I guess.'

Norah laughed a little too loudly, causing the girl in front of them to turn around.

The day was broken into modules. The older man at the front lectured while playing a series of short videos. Calvin spent most of the day scoping out the ladies from the other stores, deciding that two in particular warranted his attention. Norah patiently waited for Calvin to notice her.

During the two-hour lunch break in the middle of the day the participants were directed to a nearby shopping centre. Norah followed Calvin out. She took a deep breath and said hello.

'Oh hey,' he replied casually.

'Are you going to do some shopping?' she asked.

'Yeah… something like that.' Calvin had never been to this particular collection of stores and wanted to shop for talent.

'Do you have time for a coffee?' asked Norah.

'I don't drink coffee.'

'Oh okay.'

'This sexual harassment stuff is pretty boring, hey? At least we're getting paid to zone out,' said Calvin with a shrug.

'Yeah I know.'

'I've never had any complains, if you know what I mean.'

'I would never… I mean I'm sure you're a perfect gentleman,' she said quickly.

'I am. But you have to be careful these days. The lines are blurry.'

'Well… I don't know about blurry. I mean… it's either harassment or it isn't.'

'Yeah, yeah. No means no. I know,' he said.

Calvin walked briskly, forcing Norah to walk faster in order to stay by his side.

'So is it true you want to be an actor?' she asked.

'No. I want to be a model. I mean… in the future if someone wants to put me in movies maybe I could head down that path. Like Emily Ratajkowski.'

Norah cursed her manager's terrible recall.

'You could definitely be a model!' she stated enthusiastically.

'Yeah I know. My agent is so shit though. I've had to resort to Instagram. But I'm building a following.'

'So the supermarket is just temporary for you?'

'Yeah. How long have you worked there?' he asked.

'Too long probably.'

'What would you rather be doing?'

Norah considered this for a moment.

'Drawing maybe.'

'Are you any good?' he asked.

'Yeah. I'm okay I guess.'

'Cool. Maybe you can draw me some time.'

'I'd really love to,' beamed Norah.

'Nice. I need some fresh Instagram content and when someone draws you it seems like you have a super dedicated fan base.'

'Oh yeah… I get that. So do you… like… have a girlfriend?'

'I'm playing the field at the moment. I'm not locked down to just one tunnel.'

'Tunnel?'

'A place to drive my you-know-what through? Get it?'

'Um… yeah. Sorry… I've never heard anyone refer to…'

'I'm kind of a trendsetter. It says so in my bio,' chuckled Calvin. 'Do you have Instagram?'

'Sure.'

'You should follow me.'

Calvin cited his Instagram handle. He was so handsome. Norah wondered if he'd ever consider entering her 'tunnel.' She'd been brave so far and it had paid off. She hoped that another bold move might yield more positive results.

'I'm just having fun too,' she said. 'Playing the field. I'd be keen to go out sometime… with you… if you'd be interested.'

'Of course you would.'

'Yeah. So… do you want to?'

'Nah… I'll pass. But thanks.'

He rejected her with such casual indifference that for a moment Norah wondered if it had happened at all. Calvin was nothing like she hoped he'd be. She wandered away from him, not knowing if he even noticed her departure. She had lunch at McDonald's and felt worse afterwards.

When Norah returned to the seminar there was no sign of Calvin. One of the other girls was missing too. She sat through the remainder of the mandatory sexual harassment seminar wondering what sexual acts the two of them were doing to each other.

The girl from the other supermarket location had actually become bored with the presentation and decided to ditch the afternoon session of her own accord. She wasn't with Calvin at all. He'd been sitting alone, sipping on an overpriced but relatively healthy juice when a woman had approached him and started to stroke his chest. This wasn't completely unusual for Calvin, who was sometimes noticed by those that appreciated his chiselled features. She was attractive, a little older, with short hair, large breasts and no bra. Unusually for these random encounters this woman started to get very physical without uttering a single word.

'Whoa. You're handsy, aren't you?' stated Calvin.

She did not reply.

'Let's go to the bathroom then,' he said, standing up and leading the woman to the shopping centre bathroom.

It was during their sexual congress that Calvin became infected with a strange alien parasite. The entity had been dormant, living inside the older woman. It had seen an opportunity during their bathroom tryst to transport itself silently into Calvin's genitalia, where it could begin the next stage of its growth. He was completely unaware of the organism, which at such a small size was virtually undetectable. Calvin incorrectly assumed that the woman's uncontrollable desire for him was due to his irresistible nature. In fact the creature had been releasing a chemical into her bloodstream that heightened her urge to fornicate, ensuring its own survival. In the wake of such a significant session Calvin found himself exhausted and returned home to sleep.

That night Norah wondered what the girl from the other supermarket had that she didn't have. She considered that perhaps it was a simple aesthetic choice and decisively dyed her hair red. Her parents were surprisingly supportive, hoping the change reflected a new phase of maturity.

That Saturday Calvin felt driven to spread his seed like never before. It was an unconscious desire that lingered from the moment he opened his eyes. He visited with several ladies with whom he regularly shared a bed, hoping to extinguish the yearning with disappointing results. After each conquest his primal urge remained. The parasite was growing stronger and dispensing a part of itself with each successful ejaculation, hoping to multiply itself within as many hosts as possible. Every one of Calvin's sexual partners that day had remained parasite free due to their insistence on using protection. The alien could not penetrate latex and died quickly without a host body.

Calvin's urges passed after he'd been with three women but he noticed on Saturday night that when he became aroused while watching a film in his bedroom he couldn't ignore it, and masturbated to completion. His sex drive was unusually high and he had no idea why. All Calvin knew was that once he was aroused he couldn't focus properly until he'd done something about it.

It was due to this overwhelming issue, and not on account of her new hair, that Calvin found himself having sex with Norah.

He came in for his shift on Sunday and after a couple of hours of mindless labour he went on his break. As it was late there were no stores to browse and no talent to investigate. Calvin sat down in the staffroom and ate a chicken salad. Norah, who had been biding her time, wandered in hoping he would comment on her red hair.

'Oh hey Calvin,' she said as casually as she could.

'Hey Nicole. You look different.'

'It's Norah...'

'Right... Norah...'

'It's the hair. You like?'

'Yeah...'

Calvin stood up from his food, his appetite changing as his heart beat faster. He approached Norah, who froze on the spot.

'Are you alright?' she asked, noticing the change in his demeanour.

Calvin slid his arm around her and then led with his tongue. Norah threw her arms around him, unable to believe her luck. Their bodies pressing together escalated things for them both. Calvin was under the control of the parasite, and he now saw Norah as the irresistible one. The staffroom sofa was the location of choice and the two explored each other's bodies. Norah made a lot of audible moaning sounds as they did, her desire for Calvin Thompson growing exponentially. There was no time for contraception and in that moment Norah didn't care. She wouldn't take any action that might derail such a perfect moment. Their intercourse was brief but it allowed ample time for the parasite to enter Norah. They sat wordlessly holding one another, Calvin's mind running at a million miles a minute.

He was connecting the dots. Calvin considered his supply of Instagram followers. So many of them were horny girls like Norah. Some had already slid into his DM's. He had a bevy of women that would be willing to help him with this problem. Calvin considered that he might be a sex addict, or that this feeling of craving sexual intercourse could be filling some unknown hole within him. He wondered if failing at his dream of becoming a model had led to this thirst for others to find him attractive.

Of course it was all because of the parasite, whose only goal was survival. The microscopic alien life form would continue to escalate his need for flesh, dividing and deploying with each copulation.

'That was incredible,' said Norah as she caught her breath. 'Easily the best sex I've ever had.'

She couldn't know what would happen next.

The first phase for Norah will involve extreme itching beneath her skin followed by some bleeding from her eyes. Her body will lose weight as the parasite steals her nutrients the same way a tapeworm might rob one of food. She will briefly enjoy this weight loss and look better than she ever has before. Her co-workers will assume she is anorexic and gossip about her behind her back. Eventually when the organism has reached the size of an apple Norah will suffer a painful death as the parasite vacates her body via her rectum in search of a larger host like a horse or a hippopotamus in which to thrive. Her actual cause of death will be internal bleeding, as when the parasite grows large enough to escape her body it will do tremendous damage on the way out. But those are issues for Norah to tackle in the coming weeks. She will deal with the future alone, as Calvin will resign from the supermarket tomorrow, never to be seen again. Management will initially suspect that she is involved but find no evidence to support their theory.

Calvin's desire to become famous will materialise when his mutilated body is found in a laneway one week from now. His parasite will burrow out of his abdomen, leaving an explosion of organs in its wake. Calvin does make a beautiful corpse though, resulting in fifteen minutes of fame and an influx of new followers. He will miss his moment in the spotlight, which ends when his Instagram account gets hacked.

The Norah of this moment lies in complete bliss on the sofa, stroking Calvin's hairless chest and smiling ignorantly. She can't believe how amazing things are.

She is happy and hopeful.

In this moment Norah feels seen.

It had been a stunning fall from grace for Donnie Cortez. His former life as an actor had left a mere twelve IMDB credits to his name. A masturbation scandal, where he'd allegedly been caught wanking in his car, had been the final nail in the coffin of his career. Before he was dropped as a client his agent had highlighted an offer for Donnie to star in a porno, which he had turned down. He was famous for all the wrong reasons in Hollywood so Donnie moved back home to New York where the paparazzi wouldn't bother him. He grew a beard and started driving a taxi.

He tried to go unnoticed in his new career but word quickly spread amongst his peers and he was dubbed *Hollywood* by the other drivers. Donnie didn't mind so much as nobody really asked him about the scandal.

He put on weight, surpassing his previous personal best. Donnie put it down to the hours he drove, which mostly consisted of late nights where the only source of sustenance was fast food. He missed his ex-girlfriend Zara. They weren't right for each other in the slightest but she had put up with him, even when he'd almost cheated on her with Theresa. On the weekends he visited his mother in her retirement home. She was now seventy-two years old and couldn't understand what Donnie was doing with his life.

'I'll be dead soon,' she'd say, 'Why can't you find yourself a nice girl and settle down for me?' Her New York accent was thick.

His mother would suggest various eligible girls that he could meet, not realising that Donnie was now far from a desirable catch. He spent money on prostitutes regularly. He favoured a girl named Honey who he went to see whenever he was approaching rock bottom. While the relief she provided let him escape his existence momentarily he was often more depressed than ever when he got back into his cab.

Just as he was setting aside some money and experiencing a rare upswing of good fortune someone vandalised his car and he had to pay for a replacement windscreen. His small one bedroom apartment was rarely occupied. It only made him feel worse to be home. One night he found he'd lost the motivation to work and he stayed up late watching infomercials. He thought they would make him tired but his body clock was so severely broken that it didn't make much difference.

At three-thirty in the morning a product caught his eye. It was an exercise machine that promised results in just four weeks. All of the excited characters in the advert were happier and more confident than they'd ever been. Donnie had never purchased anything from an infomercial before but there was something different about this product. He felt compelled to own it. He had his mother's credit card, which was linked to her account, and used it to purchase the device. When he hung up the phone his head was spinning and he was suddenly tired. He switched off the TV and went to bed.

The following morning a package arrived at his door. Donnie was impressed with their expedited delivery and opened the grey box on his kitchen bench. Inside was a gun, delivered in pieces and several rounds of ammunition. The weapon came with an instruction manual for the exercise machine. There must have been some mistake. Donnie called the toll free helpline that was attached to the paperwork and spoke to a woman about the error.

Moments later he was holding the receiver, confused and disorientated. The gun now sat inside a holster, fully assembled and ready to use.

Did I assemble this?

Donnie felt like he was losing his mind. In a haze of exhaustion he placed the gun in his kitchen drawer and tried to find some sleep.

He woke to the sound of someone banging on his front door. He stumbled out of bed, dressed in sweat pants and a plain t-shirt to answer the call.

For Donnie it felt like only a moment. He reached for the handle, blinked and found himself handcuffed to an unfamiliar table.

'What's going on?' he called out as he tried to free himself.

The room was only a few metres wide with one-way glass reflecting a confused and dishevelled Donnie Cortez back at him.

'Hello?'

A younger man in a suit, with brown hair and a goatee stepped into the room. He held a folder and a recording device.

'Oh you're ready to talk now are you?' he asked in a Russian accent.

'Who are you?' asked Donnie.

'My name is Detective Dimitri Lawsov… and I recognise you from your fisherman movie Mr. Cortez.'

'How did I get here?'

'You were arrested trying to flee the scene of a murder,' replied the Detective.

'What? What are you talking about?' asked Donnie.

'Are you purposefully trying to deceive me? It won't work. I've arrested actors before you know.'

'I'm in my pyjamas here. I feel like I just woke up.'

'Mr. Cortez we have you on surveillance… dressed as you are now… running away from the Docklands on foot.'

'You've got the wrong guy Detective.'

'Well, let's review the footage shall we?'

Detective Lawsov left the room and returned with an IPad. He loaded up a video and played it for Donnie. There in front of him, jiggling with each laboured step, he saw himself running down the road. Lawsov loaded a second video that showed him running from a different angle, with the same difficult pace, his legs straining against the concrete below with each step.

'That can't be me. I can't run like that,' replied Donnie.

'I agree that you don't seem like the running type, but that's you on the screen. You're the man that officers arrested at the scene, so you're capable of running whether you believe it or not.'

'You're wrong.'

'Look at your feet Mr. Cortez,' pleaded the Detective.

Donnie looked down at his bare feet, which were now inexplicably dirty and bloody.

'How did…'

'It's you on the video. You don't have to admit it,' said Lawsov.

'Did you say someone was murdered?' asked Donnie.

'I did. Can you tell me anything about that?'

'No… I'm telling you I don't remember anything. I just woke up… actually someone was knocking on my door… I answered it and then bam… I was here.'

'You have some gaps in your memory?'

'Yeah… I'm telling you I don't know anything.'

Detective Lawsov scratched his chin, considering this statement.

'You're a terrific actor Donnie Cortez. You've still got it.'

'This isn't an act.'

'It doesn't matter. My guys are combing the scene looking for the murder weapon that we believe you discarded. Once we find that we'll know for sure. Your fingerprints will be on the weapon and that will be that.'

'But I didn't do it.'

'Mr. Cortez, will you concede that the man in the surveillance video could be you?'

'Well… yes…' he said, considering his bloodied feet, which were causing him some discomfort now.

'Then you may have murdered the man in the Docklands, whether you can remember it or not.'

'Who? Who are you saying I killed?' asked Donnie.

'Corbin Myers. Do you recognise the name?' asked Lawsov.

'No. Who was he?'

'He was a fairly powerful man in organised crime circles. Had his fingers in several known drug rings. We were building a case against him for drug importation. So… maybe I should be thanking you.'

'I've never heard of him,' said Donnie.

'Mr. Cortez do you own a gun?'

Donnie remembered the weapon he'd been sent in the mail and the manner in which it had suddenly become assembled.

'Wait… I'm remembering something…'

'Yes?'

'I got sent a gun in the mail. I've never owned one before.'

'In the mail?' asked Lawsov.

'Yeah… I ordered something… I can't remember what it was now but they didn't send it to me. I got a gun by mistake.'

'So someone sent you a gun in the mail? And they told you to shoot Corbin Myers?'

'No,' said Donnie, shaking his head, 'I told you I've never heard of Corbin Myers until right this minute.'

'Is the packaging the gun came in still in your residence?'

'I guess so. I can't remember.'

'I might have forensics look into that too,' said Lawsov.

The Detective's phone vibrated on the desk in front of them and he answered it quickly.

'Uhuh… yeah… good. Thanks.'

When the call ended Donnie waited for an update.

'They've found your gun. You didn't think we would look down the drain?'

'Honestly… no bullshit… I don't think I killed anyone. I don't think I'm capable of it,' said Donnie.

Lawsov stared at him and smiled.

'It doesn't matter what you say here unless it's a confession. And since I don't see you telling me anything I don't already know we should call it a night,' said Lawsov standing up.

'This is total bullshit Detective… somebody's setting me up.'

'Why would someone set you up? I agree that it's odd to receive a gun in the mail. But nobody forced you to use it,' stated Lawsov.

'But that's just it! They did! I wouldn't do this! They *hypnotised* me or something.'

'Maybe you're having some kind of psychotic break… or even selective memory loss-'

'I feel like I'm losing my mind!' cried Donnie.

'You can plead insanity all you want when the time is right. Someone will be along shortly to escort you back to your holding cell.'

Donnie thought of his mother and hoped that her heart wouldn't give out when she heard the news.

'Have the press heard about this?' asked Donnie, forcing Lawsov to pause at the door.

'Yes they have.'

'Fuck!' shouted Donnie as he thrashed around to the best of his mobility.

'Looks like you're making headlines again, even if it's for all the wrong reasons. What's that saying? There's no such thing as bad publicity?'

Donnie grunted in reply.

'Mr Cortez?'

'What?'

'Look on the bright side… you'll have plenty of time to exercise in prison.'

The door closed swiftly behind him and Donnie was alone again.

TWO OF A KIND

It was nice to have the band back together. It had been at least ten years since they had played a gig, but muscle memory meant that their friendship had picked up right where they'd left it. After the band split up its members had scattered across the globe. These days it took a wedding or a funeral to get everyone out of the woodwork. Happily on this occasion it was the former. It was Riley's turn to take the leap. He was all set to marry Stephanie the Real Estate agent and disappear into adulthood, but not before a decent send off from his buddies.

Riley, Blake and Seth had gathered in the city where as a team they had devoured a mountain of meat. They fell into their old roles, each man drinking and mocking more than they should.

'A toast!' called Seth. 'Welcome to the club Riley!'

The boys charged their glasses and drank. Seth had been married the longest, having met his future bride during their first tour. He'd grown a beard and now seemed the most mature of the group, even if he wasn't acting that way today.

'I appreciate you two coming out tonight,' said Riley to Seth and Blake, 'but I've asked another mate to join us as well.'

'Who's that?' asked Blake the drummer. His hair had been longer back in their touring days. Now it had receded to a point that long hair would have looked silly and he'd opted to shave it off completely instead.

'My friend Ronnie… well that is to say my *childhood* friend Ronnie. We fell out of touch after primary school but we've recently started talking again.'

'Well he's missed the food,' said Seth, who had organised most of the day's events.

'That's all good. He had something else on so I asked him to meet us after,' replied Riley.

'So is he going to meet us at the hotel room with Kibbles?' asked Blake. Kibbles had been their roadie. He was twenty years older than all of them and couldn't eat red meat, but he wanted to meet the boys later on and had organised to rendezvous afterwards.

'He's on his way here now.'

'So Ronnie's coming?'

'Yeah. Then I figure we can all get a car back to the hotel room together and meet Kibbles. I just thought I'd better let you guys know that I don't know him that well, so if he's super weird or something I'm sorry in advance,' said Riley.

'I'm sure he'll be fine. The more the merrier!' said Blake, ever the optimist of the group.

'If things go well I'll probably ask him to come to the wedding.'

Riley's phone rang and he left the table to answer it, giving the boys a chance to talk.

'I hope Ronnie's not a dickhead, since we'll be saddled with him all night,' Seth said to Blake.

'Well, you're a dickhead and we put up with you!' replied Blake.

They watched Riley wander outside and shake hands with a thin, average looking guy in a cardigan. The two returned and introductions were made.

'Boys, meet Ronnie.'

Everyone took turns shaking hands and saying hello.

'Let me buy you all a round of drinks,' said Ronnie quickly. 'Beer? Beer?'

The guys all accepted Ronnie's gesture.

'This might be alright after all,' said Seth. 'Another guy to buy rounds.'

Ronnie was a carpenter and since he'd never heard any of their old band stories the gang were delighted to tell him some of their favourites. He laughed at all of the right moments and kept the liquor flowing. Soon everyone was drunk and feeling jovial.

They travelled back to a hotel room where the three former band mates planned on sleeping that night to find Seth had organised a surprise. Kibbles, who was wearing a leather jacket, was drinking a beer while an attractive woman set up a poker game.

'Poker? Ha that's great!' said Riley. 'How are you Kibbles?'

'I'm as well as I've ever been,' he replied and the two shared a hug.

Kibbles was introduced to Ronnie and they all took their positions at the card table. The dealer waited for them to settle before introducing herself.

'I'm Katarina,' said the brunette as she shuffled a personalised deck. 'Are you guys ready to have some fun?'

They gave a collective cheer as the game got underway. Blake was an absolute amateur but enthusiastically kept raising the stakes. He lost almost all of his money in the first twenty minutes.

'Hey Katarina,' said Kibbles, running a hand through his greasy grey hair.

'What's up?' she replied.

'Do you know where we could get some blow?'

'Sure,' she replied, 'I'm in a group chat where I can source something for you. How much do you want?'

'Oh shit… now it's a party,' replied Riley. 'I've been drug free for a few years now. Stephanie doesn't really approve.'

'Well just don't tell her!' said Seth.

'So this is what we're doing then? I thought we were going out?' asked Blake.

'Let's get fucked up here and then go out later if we feel like it,' reasoned Riley.

'Yeah!'

'So you'll need enough for five?' asked Katarina.

'What do you say Ronnie? You in?' asked Riley.

'Fuck yeah. But I definitely want to go out later. There is a strip club I want to show you guys,' said Ronnie.

'Shit maybe I'll come along for that!' added Katarina. 'I'll check in with my guy.'

The card game was halted while Katarina organised the drugs. The price was higher than expected but everyone chipped in. Blake and Seth took Katarina aside while Kibbles and Ronnie poured shots for Riley.

'So Kat… can I call you Kat?' asked Seth.

'You can call me whatever you like,' she replied.

'So Kat, its Riley's buck's party as you know. We were wondering whether or not you'd be willing to help us out with some... *entertainment.*'

'What did you have in mind?'

'Well,' started Seth, 'we were wondering how much it would cost for you to give Riley a private dance... maybe a little show?'

'You want me to strip?' she asked point blank.

The boys couldn't tell whether she was offended or not.

'Yeah...' replied Blake cautiously.

'No worries,' she said with a smile. 'This is just for Riley, right? I don't have to strip in front of everyone?'

'Nah...' said Blake.

'Well, hang on,' said Seth. 'Would you be willing to do the rest of the card game... *topless*?'

'For an extra hundred bucks I would.'

'Done.'

Seth didn't have enough money on him and had to borrow the extra hundred from Kibbles. When they'd paid for Katarina's additional services they settled down to continue the game.

Katarina went into the bathroom to change and when she returned she'd removed her top. She sat down and started dealing the cards. Seth shot Blake a look. The boys had assumed incorrectly that the extra one hundred dollars would guarantee them a completely topless dealer, not one in a bra. Katarina had them on a technicality though as she was now not wearing a top, as requested. Neither party questioned the situation but Seth was quietly fuming.

They boys were noisy and extremely slow poker players. It annoyed Seth, who wanted to win and recoup some of the money he'd paid Katarina.

'Come on boys… whose turn is it?' he kept asking.

Riley had started to fade. The alcohol made him want to pass out and he excused himself. Even though the hotel room was supposed to have three bedrooms it only had two. They had reasoned that they wouldn't be sleeping anyway and were using the rooms to store their bags. Riley closed the door behind him and lay down on the bed.

'Is he alright?' asked Katarina.

'Yeah Riley's never been a big party animal. He might sleep for a while… then he'll rally,' replied Blake.

'Let's pause the game,' she said and quickly stood up.

'What? Why?' said Seth, who finally had a solid hand.

Katarina knew that if Riley passed out then she'd have to give back the money that she'd been paid for a private dance. She smiled at the guys and followed Riley into the room, closing the door behind her.

'Is she going to fuck him?' asked Ronnie.

'Yeah I reckon,' replied Kibbles.

'We paid her to give him a dance,' said Seth. 'But Riley's so fucked up he probably won't even realise it's happening.' Blake stood up and banged on the door.

'WHAT?' shouted Katarina.

'Oi, Riley?' called Blake.

'What?' came his voice from inside the room.

'You alright?' asked Blake.

'Yeah, why?'

'Come here for a sec…'

Riley grumbled and didn't open the door. Seth stood up from the card table and pulled Blake aside.

'This is bullshit man,' said Seth. 'First she fucks us over by keeping her bra on and now she's going to hang out in there for a few minutes and keep our money.'

'She's probably giving him a dance, just like we asked,' offered Blake.

'Bullshit! She kept her top on! She's a fucking con artist.' Seth was livid.

'What's going on?' asked Kibbles.

Seth explained the situation.

'Let's just go out on the balcony and look in. Then we can check up on her!' reasoned Ronnie.

Kibbles and Seth headed for the door while Blake tried to stop them.

'Guys come on… let's give them some privacy,' he called.

'Fuck that,' said Seth.

They went out on the balcony but Katarina had drawn the blinds. There was a knock at the hotel door and the drugs arrived.

'Katarina has the money,' said Blake to the man at the door.

'Let's get her out here,' Kibbles said and knocked violently on the bedroom door.

'Drugs are here!' he called, forgetting how thin the hotel room walls were.

Katarina and Riley emerged from the bedroom hand in hand. Blake gave a short cheer and shrugged at Seth. Whatever Katarina had done with Riley would stay their secret, and the smile on his face was telling.

'How are you man?' asked Ronnie.

'Good, aye,' he replied.

Katarina and the drug dealer completed their transaction and the bag of cocaine was placed on the card table.

'As promised you guys,' she said with a grin.

'Nice one,' replied Ronnie.

Katarina opened the bag, dipped her nail in the powder and took the first hit.

'It's good!' she declared.

A fuming Seth pushed his way to the front.

'I believe that belongs to us,' he said as he grabbed the bag from her and carried it to a side table. He set up a series of lines while Katarina put her top back on.

'Are we done with the cards?' she asked.

'Who gives a fuck about poker,' replied Kibbles as he eagerly waited to snort the cocaine.

'The first one is for Riley!' said Seth, placing his hands on the groom's shoulders. 'Enjoy it buddy.'

Riley inhaled the expensive powder and screwed up his face. The boys cheered.

'Fuck me… it's like washing powder…'

'Nah it's not that bad.'

One by one Seth, Blake, Ronnie and Kibbles took their turns. Katarina lingered near the table waiting for an invitation but it never came.

Halfway through the bag Riley was wide-awake but Blake was having a bad reaction. He kept pacing the length of the room as if he was on patrol.

'I'm having a bad time,' he said over and over again.

'Sit down man… you're making the rest of us sick,' said Seth, who was getting louder as the drugs took their hold.

Riley turned on some loud music and the group started jumping around the room.

'Dance it out!' shouted Riley and he shook Blake violently.

Ronnie started bashing against the wall. Kibbles tripped over a coffee table and limped back to the sofa. Blake, Riley and Seth jumped and thrashed around, feeling young and carefree. Katarina snapped several pictures of the groups dancing before Riley dragged her into the middle of the group. She danced energetically, thrusting her body at Riley. Seth threw Blake a wide-eyed look.

Blake sat next to Kibbles on the sofa while Ronnie disappeared into the bedroom.

'You alright now?' the roadie asked Blake.

'Fuck… it's my heart man. It's racing. I'm not as young as I used to be,' replied Blake.

'You'll be alright.'

'Seth!' called Blake, forcing his friend to wander over.

'What's up?' asked Seth. 'You good?'

'Nah… I'm fucked.'

'You want some more blow? There's a bit left,' he said indicating towards the side table. Katarina and Riley started kissing on the makeshift dance floor.

'It's my heart man… it's… fucking missing something. I didn't want to settle down like you did. I thought I'd have more time.'

'What are you on about Blakey?' asked Seth.

'I feel like I've missed my chance now. I'm too old.'

'Are you serious? Mate, if you wanted to find someone to settle down with you could. You're a fucking drummer! You used to be able to pick up anyone you wanted. Isn't that right Kibbles?'

'Yeah fucking aye,' replied Kibbles.

'But I'm so much older man… and I don't play anymore. I'm a has been.'

'Nonsense man… we'll be at your bucks next!' said Seth confidently.

'You got married so freaking young Seth… do you ever feel like you've missed out on something?' asked Blake.

Seth looked at Riley, finding himself suddenly jealous of his friend.

'Sometimes I guess.'

'But you fucked around,' said Blake. 'You even fucked Annie didn't you?'

Seth hesitated.

'Yeah.'

Riley, who had been listening to his friend's conversation, placed his hand on Seth's shoulder.

'You fucked Annie?' he asked.

'Riley… man… it was so long ago,' started Seth.

'Tell me right now. Did you fuck her?'

'Yeah I fucked her,' admitted Seth.

Riley punched Seth in the jaw, causing him to topple over the sofa into the wall. The punch was a shock. He struggled momentarily as he pulled his arm out of the gap between the wall and the sofa before straightening himself up.

'Mate, I'm sorry. It was a one-time thing,' he said, hoping that the physical altercation was over.

'Calm down Riley,' pleaded Katarina.

Ronnie came out of the bedroom having missed the fight completely and wandered out onto the balcony for a cigarette.

'I can't believe you did that,' said Riley with a fire in his eyes.

'It's in the past man… ancient history. And you're marrying Stephanie… so it all worked out,' reasoned Seth.

'You think… you think we're *even*?' asked Riley.

'It's the drugs talking man,' interjected Kibbles.

'No I'm seeing things clearly, aye,' said Riley. 'You're an arsehole.'

'You don't mean that…'

'No, I do. You fucked my girlfriend? That's fucked up.'

'You're so fucking righteous, huh?' asked Seth. 'You're fucking Katarina a week before your wedding.'

Ronnie stuck his head in from the balcony and called to the group.

'What if I jumped, hey? Wouldn't that be fucked up?' Ronnie announced to nobody in particular.

'We're twelve flights up! Don't fucking do that Ronnie!' called Blake.

'Do you even want to marry Stephanie?' asked Seth.

'Why? Do you want to fuck her too?'

Riley's comment prompted the group to drag them apart. He then, perhaps unwisely, went with Katarina back to the table of drugs where they both did a line of coke. Seth went back to the kitchen where Kibbles fed him another beer. Blake wandered out onto the balcony, fearing that Ronnie was about to kill himself.

'Are you alright man?' he asked.

Ronnie grinned and nodded.

'It's fucking cold out here,' said Blake.

'Hey man... I'm wearing my beer coat. I don't feel a thing. Are we still going to the strip club?' asked Ronnie.

'Yeah... I forgot about that. We'd better go soon, aye.'

Blake walked back inside and put on a jacket.

'Hey guys we should go out. Ronnie's going to take us to a strip club, remember?'

'You want to go Riley?' asked Katarina.

'Fuck yeah,' he replied. 'Hey Seth!'

'What?' replied Seth from the kitchen.

'Who is your Annie? Who is the one that got away?'

Everyone in the room looked at Seth, who felt pressured into responding.

'I don't want to do this man…'

'No really. You can tell us.' Riley held up a hand. 'Safe space.'

'This girl called Bridget. You guys won't remember her… but I do,' replied Seth, looking forlorn.

'Well how would you feel if I told you I'd fucked Bridget?' asked Riley.

'That would be messed up. Cos she's dead.'

'Yeah but what if I fucked her ages ago… when she was alive.'

'I'd be pissed off with you.'

'And that's how I feel about hearing you fucked Annie,' replied Riley.

'Well… I'm fucking sorry.'

'Are you?'

'Yeah. I've felt shitty about it for years. Can we move past it?' asked Seth.

'I don't know.'

'Let's go to the strip club boys! I've got to find myself a hottie!' yelled Blake, as he headed for the door.

'Let's go guys, we can talk about this later,' reasoned Kibbles as he put on his shoes.

Riley scooped up the remaining drugs and placed the bag in his pocket.

'Come on then,' he said, wrapping his arm around Katarina.

'Just a second,' said Seth. Everyone stopped in their tracks. 'Katarina?'

'Yeah?'

'Before we go… I just want to know how you feel about ripping us off?'

'What are you talking about?' she asked.

'We paid you to dance for Riley… it seems like you came through on that…'

Riley smiled and gave Katarina a quick slap on the rear.

'Yeah, so?'

'We also paid you to do the rest of the game *topless*… and you didn't.'

'I did,' interjected Katarina.

'I know you took your top off but you know we meant *full* topless. I thought we were all going to see some nipples. I don't want to be *that* guy… but… you know what you did,' said Seth. 'We know what you did and you know what you did.'

'Aren't you the married one?' she asked.

Seth nodded.

'That's why he needs this so badly. He never gets to see his wife's tits anymore!' laughed Ronnie.

'Do so,' said Seth defensively.

'Fuck off,' said Ronnie.

Katarina lifted her top and bra, letting her bare breasts out for all to see. They were tanned and firm. Kibbles cheered and Ronnie nearly broke his neck stretching to get a better view. Seth was surprised.

'Happy now?' she asked.

'Yeah… I guess so,' he replied. The victory was hollow and Seth sat down on the sofa. 'I'm feeling pretty tired guys. I might just head home.'

'Come on mate. Let's go to the club. I'll buy you a lap dance,' offered Blake.

'Nah… I'm not really feeling it.'

Riley approached Seth, leaving Katarina waiting near the door on her own.

'Is this because of me?'

'Look… I've just had enough tonight, okay?' replied Seth.

'Is this because you didn't get to see her topless?'

'No…'

'Then what's up?' asked Riley.

Seth got close to Riley's ear so that nobody else could hear.

'Did she fuck you?' he asked.

'Who? Bridget? I don't even know who Bridget is…'

'No man… Katarina. Did she fuck you in the other room?'

'Why do you need to know that?' asked Riley.

'Because… we paid her a bunch of money. She ripped us off on a technicality by not going topless all night. I wouldn't put it past her to rip you off in there,' replied Seth.

'Mate, I'm happy. She did enough… I promise.'

'For real?'

'Yeah. Now are you going to come out with us or what?'

'Alright… I've got a wad of cash burning a hole in my pocket. Let's get some fucking lap dances!' cried Seth.

Katarina and the gang slapped high fives as they made their way out of the hotel room. They were all inebriated enough that when Ronnie suggested they walk over only Kibbles complained.

'I'm not as young as I used to be,' he said, struggling along.

'Come on mate! First dance is on me!' cried Blake.

They walked for several blocks, twisting and turning until they came to an alleyway. As they headed down the cobblestone path they dodged a pile of garbage left out for collection. Blake tried to nudge Seth into the heap but was unsuccessful.

'Fuck off!' he cried, giving his mate a shove.

When they were almost at the end of the alley a man in a black coat stepped out from behind a dumpster. He pointed a gun at the group causing Katarina to scream.

'Gimme all your cash… now!' the figure said as his breath curled out into the cold air.

'Hey man… we don't want any trouble,' said Blake who was at the front of the group.

The man with the gun took out a bag and tossed it towards them.

'Wallets. Now!' he cried.

The boys hesitated at first but then Kibbles threw his wallet into the bag. He caused a chain reaction among the guys as one by one they each added an item. Seth took his money out and threw it in, but when he went to pocket his brown leather wallet the robber became agitated.

'I said wallets! Not just money,' he called out.

'Come on mate… it's just my cards and stuff… you're not going to use them,' reasoned Seth.

'Do it!' he said as he cocked the gun.

Katarina cowered behind Riley in fear.

'Come on man… you've got enough,' said Kibbles.

'You,' he said, noticing Katarina's handbag hanging across her chest, 'put the bag in too.'

'No… I don't want to…' she started.

The man fired the gun in the air. It was a shock to hear such a loud noise on such a quiet night. Katarina started to cry and she tossed the bag towards him. The robber took his loot, and vanished into the night.

'Fucking hell,' said Riley. 'For a minute I thought that you guys had organised that guy as a prank… you know? To make the bucks more special… then when I saw your faces I knew it was real.'

'He took all my money!' cried Katarina.

'You mean *our* money,' added Seth.

'MY money,' said Katarina.

'At least we've still got the drugs!' said Riley, removing them from his pocket. 'And we've got each other,' he said pulling Katarina towards him.

'Ugh… fuck off!' she said and pushed him away. 'I'm done.'

Katarina walked away into the night. The boys laughed.

'Don't say a word about Katarina to Stephanie, aye? I told her there would be no strippers,' said Riley.

'Well there won't be now. We've got no money for lap dances,' replied Seth.

'Yeah… it's fucked,' added Blake.

'Well, we'll have to call the cops and report it in the morning. We're too fucked up right now,' reasoned Riley.

'Let's go back to the hotel,' added Kibbles. 'Does anyone know the way?'

'Ronnie? Hey… where's Ronnie?' asked Blake.

The boys suddenly became aware that Ronnie wasn't with them. Between them they reasoned that he must have been with them as they headed towards the alleyway as he was leading them to the club.

'Maybe he saw the gun and got scared,' offered Seth.

'Maybe. He's probably waiting for us at the hotel. Come on lads. We've got more booze in the fridge. Let's keep this party going!' called Riley, as they headed back down the alleyway together. This time Blake was able to push Seth directly into the pile of garbage, which made everyone laugh.

'You fucker!'

Ronnie was not waiting for them at the hotel. He was waiting nearby for a friend. As he approached the two shook hands.

'Well done mate, you led them right to me,' said the robber.

'Easy targets,' replied Ronnie. 'Nice job getting that bag too. She was carrying the most cash out of all of them.'

'Yeah… good job you told me.'

The boys divided up their take and were happy to find a range of additional drugs in Katarina's bag. All told they had more than four thousand dollars in cash between them.

'Not a bad one, hey?' said the man with the gun.

'Yeah. I'm glad they invited me along,' said Ronnie. 'I'll let you know if there's anything worth taking at the wedding.'

Did you find the number twelve in each story?

If you enjoyed these short stories

please consider leaving a review on Amazon.

About the Author

David Farrell lives in Melbourne with his wife and children.

He has Directed two independent feature films and has a film

Podcast called *Pod Me If You Can.*

His stories *The Last Resort, The Glove* and *Dropping the Belt* are available now on Amazon.

His short story compilation *Twelve* – the prequel to this collection –

is also available on Amazon and as an Audiobook.

His children's story *You Can't Get Rid of Me That Easily*

is also available now.

You can contact him @DaveFarrell1 on Twitter